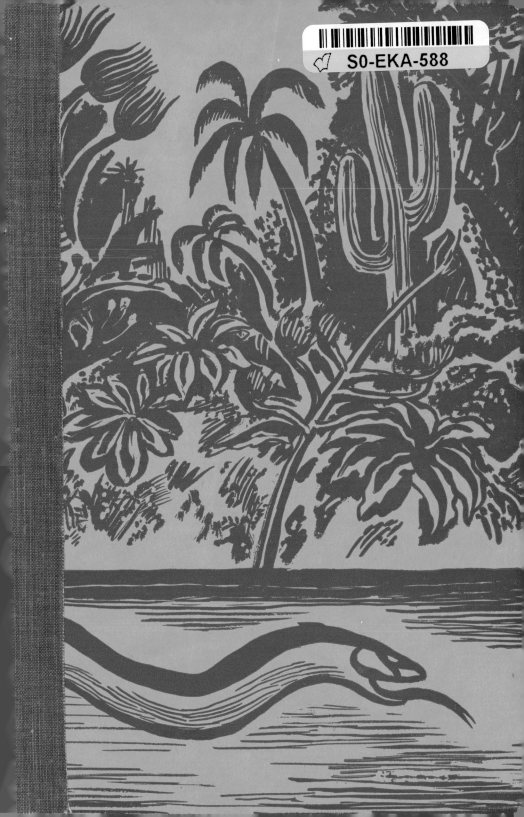

Tales from the Argentine

Books by Waldo Frank

THE UNWELCOME MAN
THE ART OF THE VIEUX COLOMBIER
OUR AMERICA
THE DARK MOTHER
RAHAB
CITY BLOCK
HOLIDAY
SALVOS
CHALK FACE
VIRGIN SPAIN
TIME-EXPOSURES
THE RE-DISCOVERY OF AMERICA
NEW YEAR'S EVE

Books by Anita Brenner

IDOLS BEHIND ALTARS

TALES FROM
THE ARGENTINE

>>>＜＜

Edited with a Foreword by

WALDO FRANK

><

Translated from the Spanish by

Anita Brenner

><

Illustrations by

Mordecai Gorelik

><

>>＜＜

FARRAR & RINEHART

INCORPORATED

ON MURRAY HILL   NEW YORK

Contents

Foreword

THE chief purpose of this volume is to introduce to the American reader a world both singularly different from, and importantly related to, his own. The stories here translated are not the uniquely ultimate expression of a literature. It would be possible, without doubt, to prepare several other volumes with different sets of tales as representative as these. And it would be possible to add at least half a dozen names to those here included, without lowering the standard and without encroaching on the most modern period, which is here deliberately excluded. The material I have chosen is both typical and good writing: I have not lost sight of the fact that any volume of tales must be, above all, good reading. But I have admitted other motives and other considerations, in my choices. It was important, for instance, that the reader should get from this volume some rounded sense of the southern nation, about which we know so little: and it was important that this sense should, in itself, serve as an appetizer for more ample knowledge. For the separation between the United States and Hispano America has disappeared: and Argentina shares with Mexico the vanguard position of cultural contact with ourselves.

All the authors here represented belong, in one way or another, to an Argentina that is past. All of them, with the exception of Leopoldo Lugones and Horacio Quiroga, are dead. Quiroga has been included, despite the fact that he is still a fairly young man (he was born, moreover, in Uruguay although he has long lived in Argentina) because he is the leading literary master of the aboriginal forest of North Argentina—that forest which, as against the central and southern Pampa and the western Cordillera, configurates the country. The forest was necessary to this volume, and Quiroga has no equal in its depiction. Moreover, Quiroga's narrative form is more closely related (this is no slur on his great gift) to the European masters of the past century than to the younger literary schools of Buenos Aires.

Foreword

A tale by Lugones seemed necessary also; for Lugones is already a classic, indeed he is indisputably the greatest literary artist of his generation in Argentina. The prosody and style of Lugones are what we call "modern," but his subject matter and his spirit hark back to the beginnings of the national consciousness. Güiraldes, a younger man than Lugones although his work is cut short by death, is also a modern, in sensibility and style; but his best work, too, is rooted in Argentina's past. He has indeed helped to immortalise the *gaucho* and the lost pampa town, whose isolation the Ford (and the tri-motor monoplane as well) has already destroyed. That is why these authors belong in this introductory volume.

For the tales here are supposed to form a kind of background—a background made alive through literary art: a background that may prepare the American public to experience less helplessly in the future the Argentine of today—the vastly potential Argentine of tomorrow. Here are some at least of the native elements that have gone into the simmering process of Argentina's national birth. The vast

Foreword

tangled jungle of Misiones is here, in Quiroga's
tale: and the jungle-mooded, mobile *gaucho* in several aspects, including that of Facundo whom Argentina's greatest man, Sarmiento, immortally portrayed in a volume of which I have taken a chapter. The more wistful, tender, profound aspects of
the *gaucho* are revealed in a long epic poem, *Martin
Fierro*, which of course could not here be represented and in Güiraldes' extraordinary novel *Don
Segundo Sombra;* and I feel that this taste of the
gaucho may justify the complete entry of Martin
Fierro and of Don Segundo a little later, in our
letters. Although Quiroga's forest remains, the
gaucho has disappeared. Before the day of the
dominion of Buenos Aires over the country, this
horseman and cattleman—wilder and more mobile
than his steed—ruled the pampa: strange product
he was of the compact, high-tempered, intense
Spanish *caballero* and of the horizonless plains that
extend like another sky beneath the sky, and like another sea beside the ocean. But it is indicative of
the literary promptness of the Argentines, that the
archaic *gaucho* lives forever in three great books:

Foreword

Martin Fierro by Hernández, *La Guerra Gaucha* by Lugones, and *Don Segundo Sombra* by Güiraldes. He is no longer a person in Argentina: he has become an essence in the Argentine human nature.

The *gaucho*, coming into contact with the pampa village, produced, of course, a rascal. And the reader can savor him, in all his archetypical crassness, in Payró's story about Laucha. If I had placed him where he belongs, in this volume, he would have appeared emerging from the unleashed physical violence of Facundo and shilly-shallying across the plain toward Buenos Aires—not the nineteenth century "big village" which the reader may savor in the episode by Lopez, but the unique metropolis which a group of brilliant young men is today depicting. Meantime, however, on the pampa, to the west and the south—between the estancias where a handful of humans huddle together within an unpopulated vastness, there came into existence the country town: stagnant deposits of humanity. And Güiraldes has given us a portrait of this town in *Rosaura*; of the over-sweet, over-receptive femininity which its harsh streets imprison.

Foreword

Argentina is a country half as extensive (if I am not mistaken) as the United States, yet in its fertile enormousness live ten million people. It is not too much to say that the Argentines are lost in their own land; and this physical lostness is symbolic of their inner state. As a national and racial organism, Argentina is not yet quite born. But there are innumerable signs that this century will witness its birth as a dynamic, authentic social being. The reason I am so sure of this is, above all, that the traits of the Argentine country are already incarnate in the men and women. This vast expanse of earth has an individual nature; and it appears already in the bodies and souls of the dwellers.

The Argentine eye, for instance, is an essentialisation of the pampa: there is something fertile, mysteriously soft, mysteriously limitless about it. There are no sharp colors in the country. Sky, earth and water fade into each other. Trees are whirlpools of green dust; rivers like Paraná and La Plata are transfigurations of the pampa. Yet in this lack of accentuated form and color, Argentina has a profound savor of fecundity. You feel it everywhere

Foreword

—on the land and in the cities. And you feel it, likewise, in the men and women. I do not know what it will be—the fruit of this fecundity. But I feel certain that when it comes, it will be both American and new.

The same unassertive pervasive fecundity exists in the sprawling literature of Argentina. Many fine writers have emerged already (this will be a literary people, without doubt—even as Mexico and Peru are essentially plastic nations). The gamut is already long, since the fluid refrains of Hernández and the Homeric commonplaces of Sarmiento. Yet for all these individual excellences, the Argentine letters give the same impression as the pampa and the people: of an expectant fertility, still subterranean or nebulous (the qualities of air and earth get easily mixed on the pampa). The most articulate part of Argentine life, one feels, is little more than the savor and aroma of what is about to come. And if something of this savor and aroma reaches the sense of the reader, the book will have served.

For it must be said that my full purpose could not possibly be filled in a single volume of stories.

Foreword

The short story is a ripe form only in modern Argentina: so that the subsequent volume devoted to the younger men, which I hope may follow if this one finds an audience, will perhaps more adequately express the country's present mood. Argentina's past traits—its transplanted European subtleties, its aboriginal crudities and new world aspirations, its feudal elegance—live more precisely in the manners of the Argentine people, in the architecture of the ranches, in the relationships between master and man, in such dances as the *chacarera* and the *tango*, in such songs as the *vidalita santagüeña* than in any short prose which I could find.

I wish to thank Miss Anita Brenner for her co-operation—far more than that of a mere translator; and Señor Enrique Espinosa, director of *La Vida Literaria* of Buenos Aires, for his great help in the difficult task of making the selections.

WALDO FRANK.

Tales from the Argentine

1. LAUCHA'S MARRIAGE

Roberto J. Payró

If these tales were arranged in the chronological
order of their subjects this one would come at the
end of the volume and the last, "The Return
of Anaconda," would be first, since it deals with
the most aboriginal dwellers of the country and
with their attitude toward the newcomer, Man.
But precisely because Payró's masterpiece is a story
of national transition, it makes a good point of departure backward into the Argentina of the yester-
days. It reveals the chaotic period when the cul-
turally still colonial Buenos Aires and the Pampa
of the traditional gaucho were, through Italian
immigration and industry, beginning to change into
the modern organism which Argentina is today: an
organism of which such cities as Rosario, Tucumán
and Bahia Blanca are the lush and noisy expres-
sions: a nation in which the gaucho rides about in
motors, and the vast *estancias* are breaking up into
small farms, worked by *chacareros* organized into
unions. This story was first published in 1906.

Laucha's Marriage

LAUCHA *—not a name, but a nickname, fitted him marvellously. He was diminutive, suspicious, restive; his mouth was like a tiny snout scantily fringed with stiff whiskers; his black eyes, beady jet, somewhat bulgy, almost with no white, heightened his mouse-like appearance, completed by the narrow small face, the receding, cramped forehead, the limp, colorless hair.

Laucha was, furthermore, his only possible name. Laucha he was called as a child in the province where he was born; Laucha nicknamed wherever

* Laucha—slang for mouse.

his fate, an adventurer's from the first, carried him; as Laucha he was known in Buenos Aires, when a recent arrival, and when no one could be traced who invented the name, and Laucha old and young called him for thirty-one years, from the time he was five, till he died at thirty-six.

From his own lips I heard the tale of the supreme adventure of his life, and in these pages I have taken pains to repeat it exactly as it was told. Unfortunately Laucha is here no longer to correct me if I err; but I can swear that I do not swerve many centimeters from the truth.

I

Well, sir, after I'd gone about for some years in Tucumán, Salta, Jujuy and Santiago, earning my dog's life as God would have it, sometimes as clerk, again as a peddler, today a peon, tomorrow a schoolmaster, here in a village, there in a city, yonder at a farm, beyond that in a plant, poor always, always seedy, hungry some days, every day broke—I began finally to figure it might go better in Buenos Aires, where it could never go worse, because the prov-

inces are never much good for men like me, with not
a peso, nor much learning, and not much strength
. . . nor very anxious to work either. . . . And
I figured and figured till at last I decided to beat
it and I began to save up by the penny—I who
had never scraped any silver!—till I raised
what I needed for the trip—the price and no
more.

I shan't go into the miracles and the tight fits I
got through to scrape up the shekels; you can imagine, and if not, it's nothing one way or another.
Anyhow one day I tucked myself in the train—
second class of course, since there wasn't a dog's
ticket!—I landed in Córdoba, took the Argentine
Central, and in Rosario sailed for Campana in the
ordinary boat, as it came out cheaper. . . . Campana was the port of call then for the boats from the
Paraná and there one took the train for Buenos
Aires.

I got off with my baggage, which was a thick
woolen poncho, native, one of those handwoven
ones, just full of the rainbow, that I'd won at the
bones from a Catamarcan peon in Tucumán; his

wife had made it in who knows how many years. . . .

Ah! I'd dropped my last cent in the meals and the sips on the way, so that in Campana I was up against it if I was going on to Buenos Aires. I'd have to pawn or sell something. Believe me this has nothing to do with my wedding; but wait! want, like the cranky hag that she is, drives a man to anything. Me, she got into marrying; you'll see how it was.

II

Well, then, I went from store to store trying to sell the poncho to get a ticket with the coin, but I hadn't a break and didn't run into a single taker.

"Those ponchos aren't worn here," one would speak up.

"I've got too many ponchos already," another would say.

"Don't buy old clothes," one Spanish storekeeper who had about nothing but nails from the time of the Flood, yelled furiously.

Finally a fellow gave four nationals for it—and I

say nationals because they'd already changed the old coin—*bolivianos*, or little-calf pesos—so gorgeous and good for a lot.

The second-class ticket from Campana to Buenos Aires cost then around a peso and a half or two pesos, not like now when they charge nearly five. So I was fixed, after all, thanks to the little Catamarcan poncho. . . . But my filthy luck, which never will turn in this lousy life, played so that while I was trotting around peddling the poncho, the train up and left without me . . . you see, I hadn't a watch, and if I did I couldn't have beat it without ticket or coin. . . .

The worst is that in those days there wasn't more than one train a day, and I had to stay in Campana, and eat and sleep at a grog-shop-inn—hang-out of the cowboys who herded at the stockyards. The lot nicked me a peso and a half, so that I was left teetering. Look what a shave!

That night I hung around the cowboys' table where they were scratching the itch for a game. My eyes popped, but they played heavy—five pesos a stack. . . . Think of it! . . . I wasn't going to ask for half a stack, naturally! . . . So I swallowed it and went to bed.

Next day I parked in the station half an hour before train-time . . . and I didn't miss it that time. But—and look if I haven't got reason to talk of my dog's luck!—I got down at one station to have a drink, and when I noticed, the train was screeching like everything five blocks away!

No, don't laugh at me: I wasn't even chipper, though another passenger had a bottle of gin—Key Brand (and not like it is now) and every once in a while he let me give it a kiss. . . . All right, all right! however it was, the thing is that I was left at the station of Benavidez, that didn't have—not by a long shot!—the folks it has now. I went back, pretty glum, to the store in front of the tracks where I'd been, which was a stand with four crazy bottles, an old native cheese, a piece of mouldy quince paste, and half a dozen sausages with a lot of canned sardines. . . .

I started to talk to the store-keeper, and pretty soon we were pals. I stood him to a drink—because I still had a few cents—and when I told him how poor and down and out I was, he told me that the farms around were looking for peons for the maize and that, like as not, they'd take me if I wasn't too dumb and didn't curl up at standing in the sun all day. To be sure, I wasn't born for anything but desk-work, the kind where you do nothing, sitting all day in the shade—but need has the face of a heathen and so that same day I tied up with a farmer who took me from Conchas, where the station of Benavidez is, to Pilar to harvest the maize.

What would you expect! In two days I was done, melted down by the sun and down and out with the brute work. I got two days' pay from the farmer, who sliced off a few cents like the good *gringo* * he was, and beat it to Belen, which was right by, looking for a better fit of a job, and there the jig began . . . or there it went on, because it had already started before. . . .

I didn't gather much moss in Belen. Before the week was out I had drifted along, and I went on from town to town and from farm to ranch, getting farther and farther from Buenos Aires, as if I'd

* Gringo—slang term used in the Argentine to mean foreigner.

9

never in my dog's life thought of looking that place
in the face. That's luck, that plays with a fellow
like the wind with a leaf.

III

Bright and early one morning I was standing in
a store, pretty far to the southeast, nipping the beast
with a drink of Paraguayan sugar-cane brandy, and
I started talking to the boss, because I was the only
customer and he was bored as me, hanging on the
counter on the other side of the plank, with his face
half asleep in his hands. I was out of a job again
and the coin was low. . . . It's that I can't stand
to be bossed, nor to shed the kicks like a mule. . . .

"Where does that road go?" I asked the store-
keeper among other things, pointing with my left
—I had the glass in my right—to a trail that went
south.

"To Pago Chico. That trail goes straight for
about six leagues, and ends up at the railroad station
of the Pago itself. . . ."

I had heard tell of that outfit, and I got to feeling like going there, just for the fun of it: after

all, working there was about like working anywhere else, and a good glass of gin would taste the
same. But as I hadn't a horse nor where to get one,
and six leagues afoot is too much of a tune, I asked
the store-keeper if some wagon or hack wouldn't
turn up that would take me.

"No, friend," he answered, "those trails were
tracked by the sheep that were herded to Buenos
Aires, but for a year they haven't gone, because the
train takes the freight."

"*Caramba*, friend, what a shame!"

"But look what a break," the store-keeper went
on after a while. "I hadn't remembered, man!
You're lucky, because this very day, or at the most
tomorrow, the wagon comes from the dealer in town
that supplies all the stores of the road to the Pago,
and mine too."

"And?"

"The driver will take you, if you get friendly
with him."

"That suits me! I'll just wait, because I've sure
got a feeling I want to see Pago Chico. It's a big
town?"

"Pretty big."

"And it has desks and stores?"

"Sure it has!"

"Fine!"

And I stayed there taking a drink now and then with the store-keeper who was a good Spaniard gone creole; till about ten that morning, a little black spot that got bigger and bigger in the green fields came up over a rise.

"See that?" the store-keeper asked me. "Know what it is?"

"Yes, the wagon! The thing is if the driver will take me. . . ."

"Don't worry about that, he's a good, sociable boy, and anyhow, if you rub him the right way, you'll have him round your little finger. . . ."

With that, and though my coin was left teetering, I bought supplies for the trip, sausage, cheese, crackers, cigarettes, matches and . . . that's all . . . though maybe I did ask for a couple of bottles of red wine. . . .

The wholesaler's driver came along, and after a few drinks and a little chinning, he had no objec-

tion to taking me, just as the store-keeper had said.

The man was a talker—I'm not so slow—so that the gossip began as soon as we left the store . . . not counting the cocktails inside. . . .

He was going back light, the horses were good, it got dark late, and so we could get to Pago Chico that same day.

I told him my life; he told me his since he had come over from Spain: always behind the counter, not going out even on his birthday, till they made him distributor, and he went around like a pup un-leashed, trotting in the wagon, and taking two and three days to get back to the Pago. When I talked about how I was looking for a job, he said:

"If you want to work without getting saddle-sore, I know what will suit you. I'll drop you a league from Pago Chico, at Doña Carolina's store, and you might grab off something there."

"That's grand, friend! I'm ready for anything, so far as a job goes, and more if I've hardly a cent left, like now. . . ."

"Then, Doña Carolina is looking for a clerk that suits her. . . . But she's very particular, and a

15

bunch have tried it and missed. . . . That's why nobody goes now. Anyhow, you'll find work, because the Torres ranch right near there always needs peons. . . ."

We ate, trotting and galloping along; I snatched a nap and woke up with the bumps; we talked some more, had a smoke, a few drinks; finally, about afternoon we got to the place he was talking about, and got off.

IV

The house was pretty large, with a business of clothes, groceries, and a little hardware. It also had a counter for drinks, with a big iron rail but no tables, nor benches, nor chairs either, so that the natives and gringos, having no place to sit, would beat it right after they'd drunk to the morning or afternoon.

We went in and a woman over thirty came out on the other side of the grate—afterwards I found out she was thirty-four—pretty good-looking still, tall, white, black-haired and with very dark eyes. When she answered our good-afternoons, I noticed she was Italian.

"Doña Carolina," the driver told her, "here is a stranger who has had bad luck, and as he wants a job, I've told him that maybe he'll get it here. What do you think?"

"Yes," answered the woman, looking hard at me; "if he stays around, today or tomorrow at the latest, they'll come from the Torres place. . . . They may take him. . . ."

"And you, Doña Carolina, why don't you take him as a clerk? He's a bright boy and could help you a lot."

"Oh, I!" said the gringa with a sigh, "I don't think about that any more. I've dropped the idea."

"That's all right," I said, "I'll stay and wait for the Torres people. And, meanwhile, will you give us a couple of glasses of good wine, because my tongue is just hanging, I'm so thirsty, and as to my friend. . . ."

We had the wine, which was pretty tasty, and the driver went off because he was in a hurry to get back to town. I hung around, looking at the house, to kill time. The store was pretty well stocked, with plenty to drink, cans of preserves on a shelf, sausages and bacon hanging from the ceiling, cheese and quince paste in a show-case, together with chunks of delicatessen, stick candy, old bread and crackers.

There was hardware too, bridles, daggers, knives, shears, axes, washtubs and pans and a lot of doodads, and on the other side of the grating, things like in a regular store, domestic chintz, burlap, ponchos, shirts, bandanas, drawers, chaps, thread, twine, pale blue and red silk handkerchiefs, and I don't know what all.

The house was a big shed with an iron roof, and in the back had a little room I thought must be Doña Carolina's bedroom. Outside about ten yards off and cornering with the store and the hitching-rack around the kind of little patio of hard ground, there was another shed, bare, and with nothing but a fireplace in the middle made of an old wheel-rim, and full of ashes; there wasn't a bed, nor anything to sit on, but it was the *accommodation* of the strangers who stayed over night. It's nothing to any man of the open, who makes a bed out of saddle-blankets; but me, with nothing more than what I had on my back, and no cover, was in for a bad night if the Torres fellows didn't turn up. . . .

I was quite surprised to see nobody but Doña Carolina in the house, nor in the shed, nor anywhere near. In the corral there was something like six or seven little curs and a reddish horse which, at first glance, was old and tame and must be Doña Carolina's mount.

Outside of the store hung a haunch of fresh meat, and a cloud of flies flew around it and others had settled and were tainting it. But I looked everywhere, and no use, to find somebody: I didn't see a soul.

How can that poor woman live here so alone? I thought. The dogs aren't enough protection, because any rascal could butcher them, and then her, and steal her last rag. . . . It's her looks . . . ! Unless the folks have gone to town . . .

I was getting interested in the gringa, so I went back to the house and I asked her:

"Pardon me, Miss Carolina; but are you all by yourself, here, in this place?"

"Yes," she answered. "We're just me, and an old

man who is over there by the creek, taking care of the hogs. He's the one who helps me out a little."

"*Caramba*, señora! And aren't you afraid to live so far from town, all alone? Because the old man mustn't be much company . . ."

"That's the way it is, the poor thing is pretty old. . . . I have a shotgun, and I can use it, but sometimes I do get afraid. . . . That's why I thought of getting somebody to keep me company and help me clerk . . . but, what can you do! . . ."

When she said that, she looked at me very seriously, very closely, and afterwards kept quiet.

"And why haven't you done it?" I asked her at last.

"Eh! Why! why! . . . Because those that wanted the job didn't suit me . . . and as I can't pay more than fifteen pesos a month. . . . Only those that aren't much good will work for that now, even if they get room and board. . . ."

Then I, half serious, half laughing, said: "And am I too one of those that aren't much good?"

"Oh! Not you! . . ." she answered, looking me in the eye.

"And then? Didn't my friend the driver tell you? . . ."

"Yes, they say it, and then . . ."

"Well, look, señora, as for me, I'd work with you, I'll say I would, for that price . . . and even for a lot less . . . I am tired of rolling. . . . The thing is, I haven't any letters of recommendation nor do I know anyone in the Pago except the driver . . ."

Doña Carolina looked at me again awhile, and didn't say a word. I'm not handsome, I know it, but I have something, something that makes me attractive, especially to the ladies. You laugh? Oh! . . . Well, if I were to tell you. . . . Anyhow Doña Carolina must have thought I wasn't so bad because pretty soon she said:

"If it were only letters of recommendation, it wouldn't matter, because you haven't the look of being a bad fellow, on the contrary! . . . But, why should you want a job like that, when even as a peon you could get two or three pesos a day, at least?"

So I told her then that I was more of a city man than farmer, and that I didn't like working in the

wind and the sun, as I'd been having to do to keep
from starving ever since my luck went bad and I lost
the little I had. I told her they fired me from a
little job in Buenos Aires on account of the intrigue
of a treacherous companion who wanted the place;
that afterwards I was through the interior, wandering around and chasing my luck, but that everything turned out bad till I had to make tracks with
one hand in front and the other behind. All in all,
I gave her one of those stories that won't leak and
she listened very much interested and attentive:
maybe she even dropped a few tears. . . .

Just then some teamsters came in to have their
drink and I went out to the patio.

They were in a hurry and left right away. Doña
Carolina let out:

"Well," she said, "if you want to stay a few days
to try it . . ."

"Try it nothing! If I stay, it will be for the
rest of my life!" I answered bright as anything.

"Maybe! . . . Anyhow, for the present I'll pay
you the fifteen pesos, and afterwards . . . if business is good, we'll see . . . I'll give you a few

clothes, you have your board, and you can sleep in the shed, I'll lend you some wool for a mattress and a poncho to cover up with."

And at that I just purred.

V

When I went out to the patio again it was almost dark, and I met the old pig-herder who had come back at sundown. He was pulling on a black cigarette, sitting on a cow's skull, at the door of the shed, through which one could see the blaze of a wood fire and smoke so thick that it hid the walls.

"Getting some air, my friend?" I asked him, to open the conversation.

"Just that, boss," he answered; "meantime the water boils and the chunk o' meat half sizzles. Want to come in an' suck on a *mate*?" *

"With great pleasure, my friend Don—"

"Cipriano, your servant," the old man put in, taking the black fag out of his mouth and just looking at it, as if he were heart-broken it didn't last longer.

We went into the shed. By the fire, which burned with a great blaze and a snapping of green wood, throwing off thick bitter smoke that brought tears to your eyes, a great sooty pot was boiling; near it was the enormous square wooden herb bowl, half full of *paranagua*,† mixed with the *mate*, of a good leaf. At the blaze itself a piece of meat was roasting, from which the salting bag hung. The old man was good to himself. He dragged in the cow's skull, I sat on another, and we began to suck and stir up the *mate*.

"And where you bound for, friend?" Don

* The South American tea is prepared in a small gourd, called *mate*, and sucked through a tube made of silver or some baser metal. By association, the drink itself is popularly called *mate*.

† A native herb.

24

Cipriano asked me, offering me a fresh drink. "Because you're not from the Pago, I suppose?"

"No, I'm not from the Pago, but I will be," I said.

"Aha! That's fine! And where you thinking of working? . . . if you'll allow me to ask."

"Right here. I'm staying to help the lady."

"Good for you! The poor thing was needing it, since the deceased went, a year come the branding. . . . A woman oughtn't to make it alone, after having pulled in a team. . . . Alone, she gets spoiled, and won't even do as a plug."

At first I didn't understand very well what the old man meant, but the hint was too clear for me not to tumble finally. Rubbing my eyes that burned with the smoke, I said to him nicely:

"Alone! . . . Not so alone, seeing as you're here."

"Maybe the smoke's in your eyes, friend, that you can't see how hobbled the years have got me. . . . Why, it's been lamb's wool and a puff and a chaw, with me oldish and stiff in the withers! . . . So quit the kidding, youngster!"

I got to laughing. The old man kept quiet

awhile, and then went on with his stories about the Doña.

"Since the deceased went, God keep him, Doña Carolina's been bread that don't sell. The gal . . . because she's youngish still—needs something, that's plain! And the fact is that though she works hard and is up with the sun, still the outfit is too much grind for her by herself, poor thïng. . . ."

He sucked at the *mate* peacefully, and went on:

"And she has a good heart . . . When the deceased was alive, it was all petting and little snacks. . . . Now, she drags in stray pups and treats them like kids. . . . As to me, with her I've got nothing to ask, and that being what I am, a broken-down plug not worth dragging to water. . . . And she does a lot of charity, too; there's not a ranch anywhere near where they don't love her like holy bread. . . ."

"I'm glad to work for a lady like that," I said, "and if that's the way it is, I'll stay for life."

He looked at me with a little snicker, and after a while went on, while he lighted a tallow candle:

"Look here! . . . As to you, what you ought

to do, youngster, is to get in right, and rub her down nicely, but with no offense, naturally. . . . You don't look so dumb, except for what takes sweat, and she, poor thing, needs company. . . . Listen to this old man that hasn't snored all his life, and take his poor advice, and see how fine it turns out. . . . And now, let's put down the grate and salt down the chunk, to finish it up. . . . You'll see what a roast! It's not much more I can do."

I took out the knife and looked around where to sharpen it, thinking on what the old man Don Cipriano had said, and I was pretty much interested. Fact is, here might end my bad days, and no harm done, and I'd begin a quiet honest life with a good woman, and always a few pesos in my pockets, easy and pleasant work, a drink when I wanted, plenty to eat, a soft bed . . .

"She's wanted none of those that turned up," old Cipriano said. "And if she took you in, that shows you've got half the way gone already. Pitch in and don't be afraid, young man!"

I was going to answer, when I heard Doña Carolina calling me from the store:

"Eh, young man! Come here, please."

I hadn't told her my name yet.

I went out towards the store.

"No!" Doña Carolina called. "Come in through the patio, we two are going to eat here inside, at this table."

She had laid a nice clean table-cloth, two places, a lot of plates, bread and butter, fresh cheese, an opened can of sardines, and a big dish of nuts and raisins.

"We eat poor man's style here, and I hope you will excuse it, as we can't make a lot of things."

"Don't say so, señora!" I answered. "If you had seen the messes I've been eating, and the maize porridge in the north, you wouldn't think so. Often I've gone through the day with a cracker and a drink, and sometimes without the cracker. . . ."

"Poor boy!" Doña Carolina said, half sad, her eyes watering a little, like mine in the smoky shed. "But from now on, you will always have what you need, for, thank God, we don't starve, here . . ."

And that night, at least, it was true, because we had noodle soup, the sardines, a meat salad, roast, the cheese, the nuts and raisins, and I don't know what all, till I had to say enough, when she began on the second bottle of wine that we had opened with the driver. . . .

Why go into the conversation, while we ate, or tell about how happy I went to bed, or how well I slept that night on a pile of nice clean sheepskins and hides . . . and even with sheets!

VI

I got up with the dawn, grabbed the broom and started sweeping the store and the porch of the house, because Doña Carolina was still asleep inside.

All of a sudden she came out, took the broom away, as if she was very angry, and said:

"I don't want you to do that! Instead, attend to the business; straighten out the drinks and afterwards . . . Can you write?"

"I should say so, señora! and I have a pretty neat hand."

"All right, that's good. Then, you are going to fix up the account-book."

"Perfectly, señora; whatever you say! But I

29

don't mind sweeping, so that if you want, I can do all those things, because the mornings are long yet."

"No, no, just the business; I will come and help you in a minute."

Eh? What about it? What do you say? The first moves were well played, don't you think, eh?

I went into the store, had my morning snack, better and bigger than usual, and started straightening out the bottles which were mostly imitations made at the dealer's at Pago Chico, and some awful mixtures. At that, I thought of a new thing that ought to turn out well. When I finished with the bottles I looked for a new account-book, and began to copy out the old one which was all dirty and messed up and handled, and full of scrawls and blots. I wrote to the queen's taste, and was already finishing when Doña Carolina came in, and she just looked at me with her mouth open and full of amazement, almost scared that I'd leave her. To surprise her still more, I told her over my cigarette:

"Do you know, señora, what I've thought of? That, as I know how to manufacture cognac, make two gallons of wine out of one, imitate bitters, absinthe, anise, and all the rest, and also mix good *mate* leaf with bad without its being noticed—we can do all these things here. You would get a lot more than now, that you're just giving your coin away to the dealer in Pago Chico."

Doña Carolina's eyes flew open, she laughed a little, but she didn't agree right away.

"It is so difficult! You need so many things!"

"Don't believe it, señora, it can be done with very little."

"It doesn't matter, for the present; afterwards, we'll see. There is plenty of time!"

But I had already gotten her good will and she half leaned on my shoulder, to look at the beautiful account-book again.

Things went so well, that the lunch that morning was even better than the supper of the night before; besides stew, we had chicken with rice, omelette, pudding with milk, and quince paste. She was won, or nearly.

Then began a fat life, chewing the rag and drinking with the customers, turns at the cards, picnics

and serenades, trips of a whole day to the Pago, on
the old horse.

"Have a good time, have a good time, it's all
right," Doña Carolina would say; "you're only
young once; and if you don't let down on your
work . . ."

The fact is that the gringa didn't talk exactly as
I say. One could tell she was Italian, by her accent.
. . . But that doesn't matter. I amused myself and
had my fun without having to bother with anything.
So what difference does the accent make? I can be
exact when I want to—and if not?—but I'd rather
make myself understood . . .

Well, then, as everything was going so well, I
thought I'd try the gringa. For some time I'd been
herding her in, but I couldn't get my proposal right
and I was scared of getting the air. . . . Finally,
that afternoon I said to myself: "Friend Laucha,
[I've also gotten used to the *Laucha*] friend
Laucha, as to this play, don't you miss it." And
that's how it was . . .

When we were finishing eating, I got the chance
and I said: "So ever since you were widowed, Doña

Carolina, you've been alone . . . all by yourself?"

I talked with a kind of a shake in my voice and looking sideways.

"More than a year!" and the gringa sighed.

I caught that ball: "What a pity, and so young!" then right away I eased up: "And so beautiful!"

The truth is, Doña Carolina wasn't bad-looking then, and she was big and fat, the way I like them, maybe because I am like I am, short and skinny.

"Well! Such is life!" she said, sighing again, and as if she hadn't caught the bouquet. "And all alone I shall be till I die, because who would have me, old and ugly as I am?"

The gringa had waited to get the compliment again, but she left me a pretty wide margin for my ends—and hers.

"Señora!" I answered, puffing my fag and very strained, "you have a better position than I, but if not—and pardon my boldness—I would swear I could make you happy—and you would forget the dead. And, do you know why? . . . because the minute I laid eyes on you, I found you charming, and now I love you with all my soul . . ."

Tales from the Argentine

Doña Carolina bent over her plate, as if to go on eating—but she didn't, and after a while she said slowly, as if afraid I would take it seriously:

"Let us drop the matter."

I kept quiet, because there was no use winding the spring too tight, and it was better to pass for a slow one. . . . She was the one to talk first, when she dished the dessert . . .

"Tell me about yourself . . . of your life," she said. "You know I like to hear you talk."

"My life has been so sad up to now, Doña Carolina! . . . Just one thing after another . . . I have suffered a lot and I don't like to bother you with my tales . . ."

"All right," she answered, half pained, "I don't want you to be sad again." And brightening up, she went on: "You shan't have to starve again, because you won't be a clerk all your life here. . . . You are a worker, even though you like a good time . . . I shall make you my partner: you know that we get our little profit here. You see how every night I take thirty and thirty-five pesos from the money-drawer, and that isn't counting the credit and the coupons . . . But, if you yourself make the drinks, which are the things that cost most, then we would make a lot more."

"That's fine, señora!" I said with eyes like a lamb's.

"Then tell me what you will need," she went on, "and I will give you the money, so you can go to Chivilcoy, or to Buenos Aires itself, if that's better, and bring it all . . ."

"Look, Doña Carolina, you make me cry, you're so good to me! and believe me, you won't find me ungrateful!"

And I went through the business of wiping my eyes with a pale blue silk handkerchief—oh, boy! —that she'd given me in the first days and that I had kept very neat and clean. Then I went on!

"All right, señora! Right away tomorrow I will go, if it is all right with you, and with two hundred pesos I'll make the trip and buy the things and mixtures I need. And in a year, you won't have to buy anything from the scoundrelly dealer except soda and beer . . ."

"That's fine! Tomorrow you will go."

I thought of edging up when I saw her eyes shining, but then I thought maybe she might buck . . .

After all, I am a little slow . . . though not so very! . . .

VII

That night everything was arranged and agreed on, in regard to the manufacture, and as to the rest, it was well started, for the gringa didn't seem to be sore about it.

Ah! I forgot! She also told me:

"You have no capital, and here there's an investment of a few thousand pesos. But we will consider it half yours, so as not to complicate matters."

I beat it, tickled to death, to the shed, where I slept, but though my bed was pretty soft, I spent nearly all night tossing and turning, and didn't shut an eye.

Well, as soon as it got the least bit light, I was itching to go and with everything ready for my trip . . .

Laucha's Marriage

I took a few *mates* with Don Cipriano, who slept at the other end of the shed on a bunch of old blankets, and with whom I'd gotten to be pals. When I told him of the partnership and the trip, dancing with joy, he said very seriously:

"You be very careful, my friend, what you do in the city; and don't let the roast burn before it broils. You're fast, but women are faster. . . . Shy ones and shrewd ones alike, before one gets going, they're back already! So watch out, and don't be left standing when you've already got your foot in the stirrup!"

I acted as if it went over my head, and laughed, offering him the *mate* which we took turns preparing, gaucho fashion. Then I got up to go.

"Well, till next time, Don Cipriano my friend."

"Good luck and till next time, young man: don't take too long, for the dumb steer you know . . ."

I went to tell the gringa good-bye and she gave my hands three or four shakes, with her eyes watering, and I got on the poor brute of a horse, which I had saddled and ready, and with its rat's gallop we got to a store near the station of Pago Chico, where

37

I left the hack very nicely taken care of, and I enjoyed a few brandies because it wasn't train-time
yet . . .

In Buenos Aires I bought labels of all the names
and all the brands of drinks, and corks, sealing-
wax, capsules, extracts of everything, and some
demijohns of very strong alcohol, because that's the
main thing for liquors. And I didn't forget aniline
powders for colouring, nor a bunch of herbs and
drugs I needed. I also bought, in case I had any
use for it, a "Distiller's Manual," and without losing
time, remembering Don Cipriano's good advice,
went back to Pago Chico, and right off straight to
the outfit "La Polvadera," as they called her place.

I won't go into how Doña Carolina received me,
but I can say it wasn't so bad. . . . No! I should
say not! the thing hadn't gone that far yet! . . .

Well, then, on the very next day, I started fixing
my mixtures, and out came anise, cognac, gin, port,
even vermouth; I drained all the wine (except a
few demijohns for our own use) and put in a lot
of alcohol, a little aniline, and out of each gallon
I got more than two, as I'd promised my gringa.

And I remember that I got so pleased with it all that I even invented some liquors, or rather, the color, and so I had blue peach brandy, gin yellow as gold, orange, green and red bitters, and a sweet little vanilla liqueur, coloured pale violet, that the cowboys used to give their sweethearts because it was so delicious, and especially so pretty.

The thing turned out grand, and the customers even liked my drinks better than the regular ones —maybe because they were stronger. And so they'd say:

"Eh, boy! A brandy . . . of the kind the boss drinks, eh!"

Carolina was dying of joy and so one day she said:

"You have the touch of an angel [only she mispronounced it] and we're making a lot of money. And . . . shall I say it? What I needed was a young man like you. . . . And now that I know you better . . . I can promise that . . . that we shall be happy in every way. . . ."

I hadn't mentioned the serious matter again, but all that time I just looked at her like a dying calf, handled her pretty and thought: You'll fall yet!

39

You'll fall yet, my dear! I was sure that she wouldn't get out of it. And still acting dumb, I came out with this crack:

"What do you mean, señora, by *happy in every way?*"

The gringa pretended to miss it, and answered me, very red:

"We will talk about it tonight, after closing time . . . Then I'll give you the answer . . ."

I could have danced on one foot, I was so tickled.

And sure enough . . . when we had eaten, I closed the store—which was locked from the outside . . . and went in through the patio, and found Doña Carolina waiting for me.

"Now you can tell me," I began very slowly, to iron out all her doubts.

But by now there was no need for all the tiptoeing.

"Well, let us talk," she said very soberly. "But first tell me the truth. . . . Would you marry me? . . ."

I was going to answer, but she didn't let me.

"I'm a little old and ugly," she went on kind of

coquettishly, so that it makes me laugh now just to think of it, "but I care for you very much, and as I said today, we can be happy in every way. . . . The thing is, we have to get married, because otherwise . . . *niente!*"

I had never thought of any such thing, but I understood that the gringa wouldn't budge for anything, and so I put a good face on it.

"Oh, Doña Carolina! I never thought of anything else, and to marry you would be my greatest happiness!" I said.

She laughed, very pleased, and squeezed my hand, almost crying.

"All right, all right!" she went on. "Then I will give you whatever you need, and tomorrow, if it's all right, you can go to Pago Chico, to buy everything we need to be married as soon as the banns are published . . ."

And as if to clinch it even better, she said that the business wasn't but part of her mite, because she had a little farm near by which was rented to some Basques, a few pesos in Buenos Aires, in the Banco de Italia, and some other little things I'd see later.

41

"And if you hadn't a rag to your back, Doña Carolina," I told her tickled to death, "it would be the same for me, I'd marry you at once! . . . Yes! Tomorrow I'll go to the Pago, to buy a few things, and see the priest, and get the godparents, and order me a few decent clothes, because I don't want to be married looking like a ragpicker."

And grabbing her round the waist, like dancing, I yelled:

"You'll see, baby, how happy we'll be! . . ."

But though the business was good, still I was a little shy on account of the relatives and the family, who would certainly find it out, because after all I'm not just a nobody, even though I was poor as a churchmouse. . . . And so I thought of a whopper!

"Look, baby," I told her, pulling at my fag, "as you are a widow and I am a little younger, and as I haven't a cent, even to die with, outside of what you give me—it would be better if we didn't give gossip to wagging tongues; you know how bad and how tricky people are, especially in Pago Chico.

Let us get married, but quietly; we can do all the celebrating ourselves . . ."

"And?" she asked me half alarmed.

"Look! We will fix it with Father Papagna, to waive the banns; and we'll have him come here, marry us, with some neighbor, or maybe even Don Cipriano, and an intimate woman friend, as godparents, and then, when everybody knows and is used to the idea, if we feel like it we can celebrate as much as we please, and not have anybody laughing at us, nor telling this or that tale. . . ."

"Do as you please," the gringa said finally, happier than a dog unleashed. "Just so the priest marries us, and blesses us with the godparents to witness, I don't care. Do as you please! . . ."

VIII

Well, sir! I'll skip a bunch of details to tell about the priest, which is really funny, and even *me*, he left mouth open and dizzy, though I have seen a lot of queer things in this world.

This priest, who was a Neapolitan and stingy as everything, had been in the Pago a short while only, but they said he had gotten rich as anything and was thinking of going back to his country soon. Rich! Tell me, if you please, how can a priest get rich, in a farming town, even if the charity rains and the candles for the saints drip and he goes fifty-fifty with the Holy Virgin? I wouldn't believe it, and a lot of others with me, that Father Papagna was even comfortable; but the fact is he was a regular scoundrel, a crook, a friar like none I've ever seen in all the country, and I've found some very good ones, and others so-so, and others pretty bad—No! not any to compare with that one!

Father Papagna was stocky, paunchy, big-nosed, pretty grey, and with hairy hands like the claws of some spider, but fat ones, naturally! He always went around with his cassock just drowned in grease, and several days' beard on his face, so he looked like what he was, a pig! I don't know whether you've noticed people that one could say never shaved; but then, how is it that they've always got just a short stubble?

Well, and, when he went out in the country to marry and christen, he rode a bay as hairy and filthy as himself. He wasn't seen much around town, except in the church itself at mass time, or when there were rosaries, novenas, or what not. The town merchants said he never spent a cent, and even sold the little hens and chickens that the pious old women brought him. He was always whining about starving though the grease just rolled off him. Such stories went around about him! . . . A lot of neighbors had complained several times to the archbishop, but the archbishop just winked, and Father Papagna went merrily on in Pago Chico, marrying, christening, saying mass and preaching. . . . Those sermons! . . . You would die laughing. You could just hear a gargling, and the boners that he spit out half in Neapolitan, half in Italian, because he couldn't even talk Italian. When I went to see him, he was in the sacristy, sitting by a dirty table, with his hands on his belly, which was big and round as a cheese.

"Whatcha wanna?" he asked me.

"I, Father . . . I came . . . I came because I'm going to get married. . . ."

"Fine! Fine! S'ten nationalli. . . . And who

you marry? . . . Gotta pay down for the banns.
. . . Girl around here? . . . Eh! . . .S'what I
said . . . ten nationalli and cheap at the
price!"

"Wait a minute, Father! . . . I wanted the
. . . how do you call it?—Oh, yes! the banns
waived. . . ."

"S'thirty!"

"And to marry us at the bride's house. . . ."

"Sixty! . . . No cheaper."

"Oh, that doesn't matter, Father: you'll get the
sixty pesos. . . . But, when could you marry us?"

"Any time you wanna. . . . She promish?"

"She what?"

"The girl . . ."

"Ah! Yes! Doña Carolina, the widow, do you
know? Of the Polvadera . . ."

"Fine, fine . . ."

And the priest kept quiet a while, as if thinking.
Then, half giggling, he got up, came over, grabbed
me by the lapel, and said low down, so no one could
hear, though there wasn't anybody in the sacristy. . . .

(Ah! as none of you seem to know Neapolitan, I'll have him talk plain.)

"But, do you really want to get married? . . . In the parish book? . . ." he asked me.

At first I didn't get what he meant and I just looked at him.

"Why do you ask that?" I said at last.

"Eh?" the rogue answered. "Because there are those that want to get married, oh, sure, but not registered in the book. . . . Then, I make them a certificate on a piece of paper, and give it to them to keep. And if . . . but you'll keep it quiet, eh?" . . .

"I should say, Father!"

"Absolutely?"

"Look: like this!"

"Then, if the woman turns out all right, they keep it; but if not, they tear it up and get out if they feel like it, and she can't do a thing, eh! . . . I have permission to marry like that; but it's a secret, a secret of the Church . . . and also it costs a lot more than the other kind. . . ."

Permission nothing! The rascally father had

47

told me a beauty he made up "for American use" to fill his pockets faster—if he went straight to hell for it—he was in such a hurry to get back to his country and lap up the macaroni.

But, after a while . . . the fact is . . . I thought it wouldn't be so bad, getting married that way, as he said,.though I'd never have thought of deceiving the gringa, especially then, and she so good to me and so affectionate. . . . That devil of a priest tempted me, it wasn't my fault, after all; and as far as the money went it had no strings to it, because Carolina had plenty. I took him on, as it seemed to be a great protection for me, and I said to the father:

"And how much would it cost that way, Father Papagna?"

"Three hundred."

"No less?" I asked him, because there's no harm trying to get things cheaper.

"Not a cent. . . . And further, you are going to swear, by God and the Holy Virgin, that you won't say a word to anybody, while I'm on this side of the water! . . ."

"Oh, Father! I can't give you so much! And I won't pay, nor swear," I added, to make him come down.

He got half scared, and patted my shoulder, and began trying to get around me. But I didn't give an inch, and he neither, and so there we were for quite a while, bargaining. Look what a business to bargain about! I'm still crossing myself! . . . Finally, when he had let me have it at a hundred and fifty, I said:

"All right, I'll pay and I'll swear," slapping him on the belly, because by now I'd lost all respect for him. And who wouldn't!

I took out the roll Carolina had given me and began to count out. You should have seen his eyes! He almost swallowed the bills.

When I gave him the hundred and fifty, he grabbed them with his claws, in half mourning with the dirt, and counted them too, and counted them again. He pulled up his cassock and stuck the money way down in the pocket of the trousers he wore underneath, as if he was scared it would run away.

And stingy! While he was putting it away, he trembled all over, as if he was having a fit. I've never seen anything like it! . . . Then he calmed down and he said:

"All right, we'll swear now."

He took me to the church through the sacristy door, made me kneel in front of the main altar, and very seriously began:

"Do you swear in the Name of God and the Holy Sacrament and by the Holy Virgin, never to say anything to anybody about how I married you, while I am in Pago Chico or in America?"

"Yes, I swear!" I answered pretty loud.

"Put your hand on this book, which is the Gospel, and by this Cross, swear again! . . . And if you break your vow, the devils will chase you all your life, and fry you in the next! . . ."

I put my hand where he said, and swore again.

"All right! Now get up, tell me when you want to get married, and you can go."

"Today is Thursday. Monday night, is that all right with you?"

"Fine! at nine, no?"

"Very good; . . . and won't we have to confess?"

"Eh! Confess! Confess, nothing! . . . For this kind of a wedding it isn't necessary! . . ."

IX

Try and think how tickled I was when I went and bought the furniture, even though it made quite a nick in the coin that the gringa Carolina gave me. I spent it all and still owed some to the furniture man, and I got credit for it in her name, to be paid in two or three months; he didn't mind trusting me, because it was known in the Pago that I was the gringa's partner and some even said she was my mistress. People always think the worst! . . .

Well, then! we got married on the Monday I had fixed with the priest, and the godparents were old Don Cipriano and a witch, of a mulatto woman who lived on a little ranch near the outfit and always went around barefoot and with a red bandanna tied around her head.

Carolina had pulled on a black silk dress, with a lot of ruffles and trimmings, and a shawl on her head that went behind her ears and tied under her chin, and some awfully long gold earrings, that swung around on each side of her red round face, and an enormous medallion with the picture of the deceased, head and shoulders, on it. Afterwards she changed it for mine. . . .

The priest, who got there on his hairy bay, and with no sacristan or anything, gargled over us about two minutes, had the marriage certificate signed, signed it himself, went out to the patio with me, gave me the certificate with nobody looking, got on his hack, and beat it at a trot back to town, yelling:

"Eh! Wish'ya happiness! . . ."

He didn't stay for supper though Carolina invited him—and that though he ate like a hog—because of course he didn't want the mock marriage smelled in the Pago.

But he took a roast chicken with him, and a bottle of Chianti and some other little things. . . .

Carolina just shone in the kitchen, and she'd made a supper that was some supper, and the four of us—I, she, old Cipriano, and the witch—sat down

to feed and wet our whistles wholesale. Say, that was a jag! . . . The old man hung onto the wine like a hungry dog at fresh milk. The witch likewise. Carolina got happy, and I . . . well, why speak of it! . . . With dessert, old Cipriano, to clinch the celebration, hung onto the peach brandy letting old proverbs and counsels, and suckled so hard that the three of us had to hoist him to the shed! . . .

"Such is life! Such is life!"—the witch kept on chattering, staggering around and drooling, she was so tight.

After a while she went completely off her nut, and as she couldn't stand up, she had to stay all night. Next day she told Carolina she had dreamed that an angel had come down from heaven to bless us, and that this was a sure sign we would be happy. That she also dreamed she'd been given a few little chickens, and some goods for a dress. . . . The cute thing! . . .

The gringa was so tickled, because I hadn't balked any that night—and who would—laugh that off! after playing sad dog for so long!—she really gave her the chickens and the goods for a dress and I think she even tipped her a couple of bucks, so that the old nigger went off tickled to death grinning like everything and her eyes rolling to the whites.

I caught her near the gate to tell her not to say anything about the wedding, that it had to be kept very quiet.

"And who would I say anythin' to?" she answered. "I'm leaving anyhow!"

And it was a fact, because in a couple of months she went.

But, and look what a world! We had started out so grand when, bing! something had to happen to mess up the party. There's always a catch in it somewhere.

Old Cipriano, ever since we dropped him in the shed, hadn't shown up and the sun was high. We didn't notice at first, but Carolina asked me suddenly:

"Look, have you seen the old man?"

"No, have you?" I answered.

"I haven't either."

"He must've gone to the creek with the hogs."

"Don't you see the hogs still penned up? Maybe something has happened to him! . . ."

"Oh, he's probably sleeping it off; but, anyhow let's go and see."

We went over to the shed, and say! we found old Cipriano belly up, all cramped in, with his face purple, and cold as ice. Carolina got scared and began to rub him, but, gee! try and do it: the poor thing, with his jag, got sent to the butcher. The gringa began to cry like a Magdalen.

"But, what's the matter with you, baby, to cry like that?" I asked her.

"Old Cipriano . . . the poor thing . . . he was so good! and . . ."

"And, what?"

"Well, maybe we're going to have very bad luck! Look what a wedding, with a corpse in the house on the very first morning! . . ."

"Bah! Don't be foolish!" I told her, mad. "Cipriano was pretty old, and he had to kick the bucket some day! . . . It doesn't mean anything; you know . . . dead men tell no tales! . . . And, besides, remember the angel and don't cry, silly!"

She got half quieted down with what I said, but still the idea stuck in her head and she stayed scared and saddish. That's the way with women, friends: just full of their omens!

I had to beat it to town, to let them know about it. The commissary Barraba, Doctor Calvo, the police doctor, and two officers came out that afternoon. They snooped around a lot and asked a bunch of fool questions, how it was, and how it wasn't, and then they carried off the old man to slice him open and see what got him, and I was left alone with Carolina, who got sadder and more scared than ever.

"They're going to chop up the poor thing! . . . Oh, what a shame! . . . *Maledetta sorte!*"

And she sobbed and sobbed.

Look, a grown woman and such a big fool! . . . "Stop crying, Carolina, that's for children," I told her, joking. "What's old Cipriano going to feel, now, of their poking! Come on! Let's cheer up a little. The dead don't want to bother the living, they just want to be let alone. Pray if you want to, but let's eat, and well!"

Don't you think that was natural! Naturally!

Carolina calmed down a little, went to the kitchen, and we ate after closing the store, and I tried to cheer her up with a lot of jokes and even jigs, and we went to bed early. . . . From the very next day the whoopee began, after we buried old Cipriano, who turned out good and dead and nobody's fault.

The friends—and I had a lot by then—dropped like flies into La Polvadera, and I received them as well as I could.

Carolina lived with the pots and fixing up the house. We, to kill time, and with a good sprinkling of drinks, fixed up this or that game; then we had cock-fights, and even gave dances in the patio, between the gate and the store.

Of the cards and the dice, the commissary—who had given me permission, though gaming was prohibited in all the provinces—didn't take more than half of the winnings, so that everything would have turned out fine if I hadn't been bit with the bug of playing hard myself.

As I always lost, Carolina began to kick.

"Didn't I say so, when we found the poor old Cipriano, that it would mean bad luck! Now everything is turning out badly! Oh, Madonna, holy Madonna!"

And this whining and kicking got worse and worse. The gringa got sore as a boil. She tried to boss me, and we had a bunch of fights, but what could she do with me, and why should she wear my pants, seeing I had 'em strapped on good and tight! . . . And with every free-for-all I made it worse, just for fun, and I got good and pickled, and the liquor supply is what paid the piper!

On the advice of a pal, and though the gringa foamed, I had the highroad fixed up, on the piece that laid out in front of La Polvadera, and got it smooth as a pool-table. And right there I had races on Sundays, with the permission of the commissary Barraba, who got to coming at times himself to collect the tax, so that we wouldn't have any roughhouse or fighting—he said.

And gee, what a hot time! The bunch came in like everything, and the drinking and what not went on from morning till night, the cash drawer ran over with coin, and I had business and pleasure combined.

But I bought a peach of a pony, racy, and that was the end of me. . . .

A dog's luck stuck to me like a leech. I pitched into a game, and bing! out every time! At cards there was always somebody had a better hand, and, pay up! And at dice,—it looked like a curse of the devil! they got me so tied up I'd lose throwing sevens! My fighting-cocks, when they didn't turn tail and beat it, flopped at the first jump! "Better luck next time," they'd say, and naturally I'd get so sore that I took it out on everything like a mad bull.

And as here a nip and there a taste you drain the keg, the pesos flew like beauties. But I had a big hope, and that was the pony, a beautiful brute, with tiny hoofs, a long neck and a little head, slender, not the ghost of a paunch, brisk as everything, and tamer than the old hack. I fed him myself, and washed him, and currycombed him, and every morning I went out to try him where nobody could see. And with a few runs that we tried out, with just a few friends, the baby turned out a sure winner. What

61

speed! They couldn't beat me with him, luck or no luck!

Carolina with all this, seeing the money go like water in a leaky tub, began to raise Cain worse than ever.

"We can't go on like that!" she'd say, sore as everything, and half crying. "You're throwing out everything I've gotten with my work, you loafer!"

When she got real mad I'd yell too, and louder than her.

"Let me alone! You're a cranky gringa! Don't bother me, or you'll see what you get! Shut up, and in a hurry! . . . eh? Did you hear me? . . . If you don't shut up, you'll be sorry!"

I was thinking of the marriage business and the paper the priest had given me, though not of throwing her out, poor thing! . . .

She tried to hide the coin, but, where wouldn't I smell it, if I got to feeling like taking a stack, or rolling a couple of bones! . . . And Carolina, when she saw I'd snitched it, yelled and cursed first, and then she went and cried in a corner.

"It isn't the money! It isn't the money! It's

that I can see you don't love me and you don't think of tomorrow."

"Never mind, baby—" I'd answer, sort of tamed down by the tears. "You'll see how we'll get it back! Don't you worry, silly! We're going to be very happy!"

"Ah, Madonna, holy Madonna," the gringa would sigh.

. . . As soon as I figured the pony was right, I fixed the clean-up. I had him hidden, as I said, and only two or three friends knew about him, and they figured playing him hard, and wouldn't have peeped for anything.

Early one Sunday I got him, and cut his mane crooked, and shaved him in patches, and filled his tail with mud and burrs, and made him look, all in all, like the worst plug of a bunch of white trash. Then I put old mountings on him, and gave him to a peon from the Torres outfit that I'd already bribed, and told him to drop in at race-time, at La Polvadera. The peon went off with him.

"I'm going to race the pony today," I said to Carolina.

"Leave those things alone," she answered. "Race, nothing! Gambling is the road to perdition."

"This time I'll win sure! I've disguised the pony, they're going to think it's a plug, and you'll see the pile of pesos we'll clean up!"

"Promise me, at least," the gringa said, seeing me soft, "promise me that if this time you lose, you'll never gamble again."

"Look, like this!" I answered, and crossed my fingers and gave it the kiss. . . .

x

Well, what would you expect! The crowd began coming and the place got as full as the plaza at Pago Chico itself on a holiday. Several races went off. The coin ran, and we could hardly wait on them all. The bunch was warmed up like everything, when the peon got there with my pony.

There was a fellow named Contreras, who thought he had it all, on a pretty fast black, but nothing wonderful. My pony could beat him hobbled.

Laucha's Marriage

Contreras was no angel, he meant bad, fought like a jailbird, and gambled bunches of coin that he got who knows how: they said that the crooked lawyer Ferreiro gave it to him to keep guard over him, and to scare his political opponents . . . with clubbings and even stabbings if it didn't go farther.

"Your black's a beauty!" I told him, picking him for the heir, because he was a fellow to bet hard and that's what I wanted. "Pity he's got so fat!"

"Fat! Quit your kidding! He's in form, my friend, and can wipe up the sweetest! And that with the long trip we've made. . . ."

He was lying. For a week he'd had him resting in the Pago, preparing him.

"Bah!" I went on to get him sore. "When they begin to get paunchy . . ."

He looked at me, laughing to hide how mad he was.

"Don't rock the boat, there's no pump, my friend! If you want to see its belly, you've got to wear glasses. And, belly or no belly,"—he went on yelling, "where's the smart boy wants to lose a hundred pesos?"

A crowd got around us.

"With the horse in that state," I answered him with my cigarette hanging on, and half laughing, "I'll run any old plug against him."

"Listen to him! And with which?"

"With that mangy pony, no further. Will you lend it to me, friend?"

"You bet!" the peon that brought him answered. "Run him out!"

Contreras looked at the horse hard, slapped him, made him walk a little.

"This plug ain't what he looks like," he said. "Try to get by me: But . . . I won't back out. . . . I'll run, bah!"

"For the hundred?"

"And how!"

"Let's put it up!"

"Put it up? Watch out, my friend!" he yelped, rolling his eyes.

I knew that meant fight, and so I shut up, unsaddled the pony, put a bridle and a blanket on him, took off my coat and vest, tied a red handkerchief around my head, and, ready.

Laucha's Marriage

The crowd was good and hot, and played wild. A lot offered two to one against me. I grabbed a bunch of those bets, and the friends who knew about the thing, grabbed some more.

The track was a couple of blocks. We let out, and beat it, and my pony began to get in his, first the head, then the neck, then half a length, and not hurrying! Contreras came like the wind, bing-bang! . . . Of course the black was going to wilt, but he was blind-mad on account of the trick. . . . I knew the race was mine, and so as not to let them find the pony all out, I kept him in. . . . Even so I got a length ahead, when, damn it! half killing his black, Contreras caught up, stuck a leg into the pony, which goes over and drops me on my ear and then zooms past like a shot! Son of a . . . !

Luck was I landed on my feet, but what a stampede got started! The crowd came up yelling and cursing, even shoving into the judge of the race. . . . Knives came out, and if the commissary Barraba hadn't stepped in, the thing would have ended up bad.

Contreras went back to the gate, stopping a yawn,

very pleased with himself. . . . Gee, I was mad!

When he got to me . . . I was joining the bunch in front of the store, riding the jumpy pony—I couldn't hold it and I yelled:

"Crook! Sneak, scoundrel! You kicked him, you son of a . . . !"

And at that he jumped off the horse and pulled out the blade. I got back to draw mine, too.

I don't much like that kind of thing, why should I say so? I'm short, pretty thin, not very strong, and more, I don't understand the knife much. But the man was at me, the crowd was around, and I had to come through. . . .

He got two slices at me which I managed to hold off, somehow. But the bacon was burning, my friends! . . .

"Everybody get's what's coming to him!" Contreras was yelling at me, snickering and trying to make a fool of me.

I was already saying my prayers, and the brute sure would have chopped me, if Carolina hadn't landed, running and screaming, gone crazy, and I don't know how, maybe because she was so desperate, rip! she snatches the knife right out of his hand.

"And you let him, you let him!" she screamed to the crowd.

The gauchos got around us, and pried us apart, and then afterwards the commissary Barraba butted in. I had been dumb enough not to tell him about the pony, and he had bet on the black. . . . It takes my luck! . . .

Contreras, and most of the crowd, said that the black had won fairly, and that the tumble was because the pony wasn't a race-horse. . . . The judge of the race was trying to get out of it; I had no pull with him, nor my friends either.

"Let the commissary decide!" some of the bunch yelled suddenly.

"Yes, yes! . . . that's it!" all the rest who had played on the black got to braying.

And the big crook of a Barraba decided:

"The race was fair. Contreras won!"

You can't beat the law.

"But, señor commissary," I began.

"Shut up and beat it! You've got to pay up!"

And I had to pay sure enough, with my mouth

shut, and there went the last of the savings . . . and even the cash-drawer! . . .

Carolina just looked at me with her eyes popping, and she had good reason.

"My soul! I owe you my life!" I told her.

"Yes, yes!" she answered, half crying. "But don't play, don't play any more, oh, please!"

"Yes, you be easy about that!"

And I got to waiting on trade and taking a few drinks myself, to forget all that trouble, and, what do you expect! The gin got me and I started standing rounds. Look what a time I picked!

"Eh, friends, help yourselves!"

And after a while, another, and another round . . .

"What will you have, gentlemen?"

Carolina was furious.

"Ma! . . . Ma! . . ." she was saying at me mad as everything.

"The lady is calling her mamma," one of the customers said.

"She's watching the boss nurse himself!" another came back.

And then, I don't remember a thing!—I think there was music and dancing, and that I put out everything there was to eat and drink on the place.

The fact is that the store was left teetering! But then, what a jag!

The next morning, I found myself in a ditch by the gate. Maybe I slept there, but I don't know how I landed in that bed. When you get a blind one! . . .

The gringa was locked in her room, and she wouldn't open with a wedge, and, as she told me afterwards, she had spent the whole night crying like a lost soul. When I finally got her to open, she cried and begged so much that I melted, and promised that it was the *last time*, and told her I was going to start working hard, like a burro if I had to, so we'd get back everything we'd lost, and I'd never even think of gambling, or cock-fights, or races.

"Do you think I'm going to forget you saved my life?" I told her—"because if it hadn't been for you, Contreras sure would have got me! . . ."

But man proposes and God disposes . . .

Well! and what of it! It's nothing to be scared

of . . . I'm not the first that has forgotten his promises on account of his tastes. Nor the last, either . . . That's the way with man, gentlemen, and even the grandest, if he's not a hypocrite, will admit that he's forgotten his good intentions plenty of times—or those he hasn't mentioned, at least— to please himself better.

And that's everybody. But the thing is that some of them know when to stop, or manage to fix it so's they can do as they please, and play dead, and nobody says anything.

And if not!

Some of them play and soak in the clubs, and keep it quiet, and fight duels, right out in front of the police, and do the same things I did, and worse, but as it's them, it doesn't look so bad and nobody blabs. . . .

Well, to make a long story short!—The fact is, that the debts and the gaming nailed me again, and I, like a fool, played hard, and all the world took it away from me like candy from a baby! And so after the savings, went the little farm. But Jeez, what a riot that day! The gringa—would you believe it?—even scratched my face, and I went around pinked for days . . .

"Look, gringa!" I yelled. "You don't know what you're doing! When you least expect it, you'll see! . . ."

I was going to let it out about our not being married, but it came over me that she was so mad she might not sign the sale, and throw me out of the store . . . like a log!

"If I had known!" the gringa was screaming. "If I had known!—*Porca la*. . . ."

And she'd grab at her hair. But she signed . . .

Why add that the pesos in the Italian Bank had gone their way? The store was left . . . but nearly as bare as the palm of your hand . . . not a bottle, not a blanket. I'd ask myself often where it had all gone, even with all the celebrating, till I noticed that Carolina, with her cryings and her rages, neglected the business and let it sink. . . .

Then I tried to fix up things by myself; I bought a lot on credit, and began half patching the place. . . . But the truth is: the gin and the cards, and the bones and the cock-fights, piled up into a lot of bills that just began to rain on us, a regular carnival. The sheriff didn't do anything but ride back and forth from the Pago to La Polvadera, as if he'd been hired for the job. . . . And we had no one to turn to, not even the pony, which had got crippled with the fall! . . . Then I remembered what old Cipriano used to say:

"Born nigger, always black!"

Bad luck had chased me always, why should it change now?

Carolina realized that we were worse off than tramps, that they'd sell the store out from over us, that we hadn't a cent left, and one day, she sailed into me. Christ! I even hate to think of it! . . . She'd got the taste with the scratches, and she even grabbed a stick and began to hit me . . . word of honor! A beating! . . . Me! . . .

And I, what would you expect! pulled out the knife, naturally not meaning to hurt her; but when she saw me with it, she got off, but with her eyes popping, and foaming at the mouth. I'd never seen her so mad! . . . She was a regular tiger! . . .

"Scoundrel! Robber! Crook! . . . Is that the

way you remember that you owe me your life?
Give me back my money, *birbante, canaglia!*"

And I, how was I going to let her talk to me like
that, and even hit me like a child?

"You look, Carolina!" I told her with the knife
still in my hand. "I'm leaving right now and for
good, understand? I'm sick and tired of you!"

She changed her face at that, but she went on
yelling and insulting me.

"What? You leave, Madonna! After you've
left me bare and in the streets, you scoundrel, you
bum, you thief! Ah, no, *per Dio!* You're my husband, and you've got to stay, and work like me,
porca la . . ."

I just laughed and laughed.

"And who told you I was your husband?" I said
to her. "Well, it isn't so! You're nothing but my
mistress."

"You're lying, you scoundrel!"

"I'm lying? Yes? Well, you just go ask the
priest and you'll see . . ."

"Father Papagna . . ."

"What! Your *Napolis* beat it a month ago to

mangiar macaroni at home. . . . Go on, ask the new one, and see if there's any record in the church. . . ."

She just looked at me with her mouth open, as if she couldn't believe what I said. . . . All of a

sudden, she thought maybe it might be so. . . . Scared, desperate, crazy, she went out running. I saw her beat it on foot on the road to the Pago, hatless, in her house clothes. . . . She was sure on her way to make certain. . . .

I took out the few pesos that were left by chance in the cash-drawer, saddled the hack and—if I've met you I don't know you!   I went the other way, after I tore up Father Papagna's paper, and very peaceful and sure that they wouldn't go after me. . . . What?   And you let that bother you? . . . But look, it turned out much better for me . . . and for her too.

Have I heard?   Sure.   Yesterday I was told that she was fine: working as a nurse in the hospital at Pago Chico.

2. DEATH OF A GAUCHO

Leopoldo Lugones

The War of Emancipation between Spain and her
American colonies began in 1809 and did not close
until 1824, raging uninterruptedly during all these
years from Mexico to Chile. The Province of La
Plata (Buenos Aires) early achieved independence;
but the Spanish forces repeatedly came down from
High Peru (what is now Bolivia) and met the
gaucho rebels in northern Argentina. When the
Royalists (largely recruited from mountaineers)
faced the gauchos on the plains, they were beaten;
but when the plainsmen followed the mountain men
into the rarefied air of the Cordillera, they were
beaten. This savage ricochet of armies and guer-
rilla bands continued until at last the great Argen-
tinean general San Martín carried out his inspired
strategy of crossing the Andes and definitely destroyed the Spanish troops on the littorals of Chile
and Peru. Lugones' tale is an episode of the first
phase of the fight, between gauchos and Spanish
regulars, in northern Argentina where mountain
meets plain. It is one of the stories of "La Guerra
Gaucha" (The Gaucho War).

Death of a Gaucho

OWARD the end of afternoon a pensive horseman climbed over the ridge. As he descended, his shoulders, nearly covered by the wide wings of his hat, approached the level of the hill. Thus his back; but face to face, he was revealed a gaucho returning from some festivity near by. The starch, scented with sweet basil flung by the girls, silvered his hat; and on his red scarf glistened scraps of the egg-shells filled with perfume.

In his ears echoed the rhythm of the timbrels to which the ballads had been sung, and of the piping *elkenchos* which pierced into them; and the tunes slipped between his mustaches, gradually changing from a whistle to a hum.

He still felt around his waist the soft arms of the girl with whom, she behind on his horse, he had leaped the gate of the patio fence for fun and better than the others. Lovely spree, with *chicha* * and not too little petting.

To the shower of the carnival whose traces still spotted his poncho, had been added the downpour of a thunderstorm which had caught him as he climbed, delaying him; for as the clouds were violent and a gallop is likely to attract lightning, while the rain lasted he tethered.

But, though now there was nothing to hinder him, he maintained a slow pace. His gaze followed the curving trail, fixed to the ground like a file of ants. And at each step his attention doubled. Behind him the clouds, spread over the sun, enveloped the hills in cerulean shadow. To his right a cleft full of hail suggested a fleeting snowstorm.

The man, low on the saddletree, examined the slope. The shower had not reached that far, and perhaps its crags might preserve a trace of the thing that preoccupied him.

* Chicha. A native intoxicant, originally used by the Indians of the Andes.

Death of a Gaucho

His doubts were cut short by an open smile of professional pride. Traces of mules, mounted mules judging by the distinct stamp of their hoofs, pointed a trail away from his own.

Surmising the number and the pace of the animals, he advanced smiling still more broadly; for if before, he thought he had found the trail, now he knew it, and he drew from that a probable inference. It disappeared for some time over the hill in the valley that lay between it and the neighboring mound. He suspected something like that. Ten different tracks implied ten different mules. Nobody around here owned that many; therefore the riders were not peons. Neither were they his friends on the way home from the carnival, because this road was out of the way, and they were not more than six. Six, and here were ten mules. . . .

Useless to think of mule-drivers; they preferred the highway. These, then, were not pack animals, but were mounted, as he could clearly see by the straight, evenly distanced tracks.

His horse nodded in that somnambulistic trance

which tame animals acquire, homewards at sun-down. He drooled saliva upon the track of the mysterious travellers.

"They ride two by two—" the trailer muttered softly, speaking as if they were passing now. *"Here they stop . . . here they trot. . . ."*

Now and then, thunder rolled out of the earth like an enormous word.

And the tracks were not made by the mules of the region, because he knew them well for a hundred leagues around.

An idea struggled through his skull and clouded the afternoon which had become distrustful. Those horsemen, now concealed in the mountains that rose beyond, began to alarm him.

They had unsaddled in a clearing. The place was obvious where one animal had rolled: ironed the ground. And still more, here were tracks of bare feet, and not Indian, because the print disappeared between heel and toe. . . .

Ahead, a few hairs shivered on a branch; clue that the travellers had not country harness. The animal to which they belonged was dun; and the leader, a male, because the frog of its hoof was outlined a half-moon instead of a hoop. . . .

These things added nothing to his investigation, but they did confirm its accuracy.

More and more intent, the rider now climbed the slope he had faced, and one phrase described his suspicion:

"Los maturrangos!" *

The sierra which rose beyond the soliloquy, knew the truth; and towards it he turned his horse, now at the peak of the ridge.

Over the hills ridged by milky vapours, the cloud spread a mantle of mauve which the light powdered with saffron. Spirals of clear gold in minute folds floated upon it. A sulphurous yellow warmed the horizon. Under beams of greyish light, a stretch of mountains appeared, quilted a tender green.

The mists thinned; as they moved, their reflections seemed gentle lightnings. The air, at first violet, cooled to blue; paled to a white lightly illumined with lilac, and suddenly deepened to livid

* Maturrangos. Idiomatic name given to the Spanish troops by the gauchos.

scarlet. Then the bosom of the storm coagulated, like lucent grapes, flushed with carmine that above shaded to sombre purples. Narrow beams of sunlight gilded the valley. The dying fires flamed again and torridly ruddy scalded the clouds. A clump of trees in the background stirred the colour of the scene. The hill, indigo, gleamed like the bosom of a dove, and the horizon seemed a profound rosy stream.

The trailer, one hand over his eyes, gazed upon the peaks. Far away, a herd of *guanacos* * fled from cliff to cliff, and this was significant. People were there. The riders, beyond doubt. This certainly cheered him. That troop travelled briskly; he could not overtake it if he waited to get his friends the guerrillas. Then, he would go it alone—that was clear. One against ten could manage, if he were spry. . . .

He decided at once. The reins gathered in, his heels out, he still calculated the distance, the best road to circle and face them, using short-cuts. And in the sunset glare, he was the picture of terror.

* Guanacos. Native animals of the mountains, similar to llamas.

Death of a Gaucho

His nose, dented in, made his face look like a skull. Set wide apart, his little hazel eyes like a colt's shone cloudily moist. The hat was a halo. The pompons of his chin-strap, held under his mouth, bristled his little sandy mustache.

One final glance pierced into the sierra, whose dark veil had thinned to the opaque clarity of thick glass. And like this curtain, a distant shower fell from the clouds. The man hesitated a moment still, touched a heel to the horse, settled the wad of *coca* * into his cheek and took the trail. The carnival refrains continued:

> Qué lindo es ver una moza
> —*La luna y el sol*—
> Cuando la están pretendiendo
> —*Alégrate corazón*—
> Se agacha y quiebra palitos
> —*La luna y el sol*—
> Señal que ya está queriendo
> —*Alégrate corazón*—

The verses carried vague sorrow, mirages of endless liberty within endless slavery; pleas of a love

* *Coca.* The leaf native to South America, from which cocaine is extracted and which the Indians of the Andes chew like tobacco.

rising from great distress, of love grieved and lonely
and longing . . .

The sky, delicate as a shell, diaphanous rose, was
heightened by the evening star which gave it a gentle
pulse.

> Miren allá viene l'agua
> —*La pura verdá*—
> Alegando con la arena,
> —*Vamos, vidita, bajo el nogal*—
>
> Así han de alegar por mi
> —*La pura verdá*—
> Cuando me pongan cadena
> —*Vamos, vidita, bajo el nogal*—

Across the twilight, the horse drowsily, leisuredly
trotted.

The royalist detachment, increased by five, biv-
ouacked as the day came to an end. Misled by the
guide, who tried to get away when they had barely
reached the depths of the hills, the soldiers returned
from shooting him, with no trace of the provisions
they had searched for.

The rest, save one who carried half a carcass of

beef, had been equally unsuccessful. Not one came upon an enemy or a town. The guerrillas evidently neglected these regions, were concentrated, perhaps, on the main body of the troop. They would at least sleep peacefully, supping on dreams.

To their fatigue accrued four wakeful nights. Their jaded mules needed rest too. They had come all the way from the plateau of the Andes, firm and sturdily docile, but made gaunt by hunger, bled by the parasites in the woods, arching their ears in melancholy upon the gloomy wrath of the army endlessly trapped in the hills. Few mules were left, and when these broke down they were eaten. Today they had travelled since breakfast; a sign of their acute distress. That night, certain of solitude, they went to sleep with no further anxiety.

The trailer waited flat on his stomach by a moss-covered rock. Beside him four men in the same position exchanged now and then imperceptible words.

The invaders were camped a short distance away, around their stacked guns which the moon, thin still, and low in the skies, revealed. Beyond, the mass of animals stirred confusedly; another mass, immobile in the middle of the sleeping troop, located their ammunition cart. The sentinels, doubtless vanquished by sleep, threw no alert silhouette on the scene.

One of the rebels stood up and turned toward his horse which had begun to sniff and snort; he wrapped its head in his poncho to silence him; another improvised a mouth-wedge for his, with the handle of his whip. They lay down again, bit on their wads of coca and set their daggers in the sheath once more, sharp edge down, so that they would turn edge outwards when they were drawn. One way or another the others also settled themselves, and again they were still. The soil slept under their bodies.

An hour passed. The moon went down at last, and a puff of air fluttered at the backs of their necks. They had waited for it. It was the wind that blows when the moon goes, and it arrived punctual to its own whistle.

The first puff was followed by a stronger, then

another, then more. The trees murmured in their dreams. The hum in the air grew rapidly marked, increased to rustles in the bush. The breeze unfurled all its scale to pitch, the stars winked faster and a kind of dim babble rose from the fields. . . .

Five shadows slipped toward the Royalist camp, which was doubly hooded in slumber and cloaks; and shortly after, vague spirals of smoke floated around it, spread to earth-level by the wind. A few sparks ran in the grass; quivering little flames leaped a finger-tip above ground, and broke out beyond. . . . And as the wind swelled at that moment, the night burst into fires.

In the flare, the rebels swept furiously forward, on horseback, their palms to their mouths, their whips high on the battered flanks of the mules which flinging their heels to the fire disbanded.

The flames licked toward the ammunition cart, threatened the terrible explosive with the fringe of their crest of sparks. The eight or ten rubies of the blazing diadem that encircled the Spaniards fused into a single crater. Shadowy figures drawn thin by the glare leaped under the smoke, kneeling in clumps and shooting not knowing what.

One squad spread startled on the ground like guerrillas. . . . Half-nude men dragged at the powder. Shouts of command mixed with curses of desperate anger, pleas, insults. A mad bugle blared.

A ruddy shower dropped on the cover of the powder cart. The blaze ate into the bushes to the roots, fluttering with the crack of a wind-blown sail, choking its scorching breath into faces, fermenting eyes with its smoke. Whistling and laughing the trees replied to the shots of the dazed troops. The dry saplings caught with rings of blue light, burst in plumes of flames that twisted in the air like sheared wool. Frightened birds rose from the hills, small grubs spilled over the ground like dark little spools.

Gusts of wind broke the bright net now and then, and downed the smoke, uncovering pulsing mats of live coals. The column retreated before this assault of the flaming battalions that the rebels had loosed upon them, skirted one side of the fire; but the blaze bristled its quivering ridges stubbornly, lashed with it the boughs so lighted that they seemed crystal, emptied the pump of its lungs into the night. From the column, bayonets rose, and swords, black against the illumination that reddened around them in explosive waves, brightening limp braid and ravelled stripes.

Those soldiers maneuvered with such heroic daring against the charge of the fire, that the distant hills called *good!* from under their snowy cloaks.

The flames beat on their backs, pinned sparks like glowing burrs on their clothing; and while some pulled at the cart, others started a counter-fire ahead to rob the blaze of its power. Their safety depended perhaps on that barrier which they controlled at last; but the wind turned capricious. Drawn in by the oven that the fire was tunnelling, the entire furnace wheeled upon the rampart. The flames stretched like arms, caught on the other side, and the battle was renewed.

The regiments of the fire invaded the shadows wavering, left puddles of liquid carbuncle. The coruscant army was led by guerrillas, leaping goblins; behind them whirled rose swords and flamboyant banners—the dragoons; then, among sparks that broke to crisp sheaves in the air, rode, crested by bushy plumes, higher, higher, the cuirassiers in ochre; and the last phalanx, the burning trees that reared their forked brands in the dark, even higher, were the grenadiers with their coats of shimmering mail.

Swarming musketry crashed in the green branches. Muffled explosives traced their semicolon in the air. The bark peeled off in lambent shreds. And the snore of the flames surged over this riot of incandescences and veils that the troop still fed with gun-powder.

The retreat became flight. They flowed into the unknown, dragging their failure through the solitudes crushed by a ceiling of smoke so low that sometimes their heads rose above it. And in the solitude a new obstacle arose. A rough wall barred the road; in the face of this unexpected rampart their hopes surrendered. Such a plot of chance implied that sorcery was against them.

This coil of catastrophes maddened them. Some settled their rifles with supreme decision under their

94

chins. Knives began to cut into the path. Some-one appeared on the wall, standing with open arms. "Scoundrel!" they yelled, from everywhere.

But the bugle cried its message of obedience and death. Pirouetting and sidling to climb the wall, they all passed; this obstacle now behind them meant salvation; but at once they were all struck by a thought: the ammunition cart!

It exploded at the instant. And still buried in the mass of smoke that rolled over upon them, they were assailed by some formidable thing that burst over them, sowing death. That thing pierced the smoke, was lost in the distance howling. It was felt tearing once more from the shadow, again attack-ing. . . .

Now they could see him. Sword in hand, one horseman, one alone, threw himself upon them. Many raised their bayonets; but still blinded, they could not repulse the charge. The daring rider swept through them in a frenzy of swords and yells.

An exclamation. . . .

. . . Silence. . . .

. . . Again the gallop. . . .

He reappeared in the breach that the explosion had made in the wall. He rushed among them. He met the bayonets. Their shots felled his horse, but he rose intact, on his haunches, before the astonished soldiers; he ran to the barrier ducking under the net of bullets sewn about him, and backed by the stones, he waited.

The royalists stampeded, and a cluster of swords rose over him. Bush burned by the wall, so that the struggle was focussed upon it. The raised swords slashed down, and when the fighter for his country rose again, he was garbed in crimson.

But he attacked too, rapidly passing and feinting, breaking with improvised dodges, dropping to the ground to flex. They came at him so compactly that shots were impossible.

Covetous of his skin, they roared their desire in oaths, their jaws clamped by their teeth set on edge with rage. That gaucho represented with his body the insulting fire that had routed them; displayed within reach at last some rebel flesh. They were so certain of killing him, that they did not even suggest surrender.

Death of a Gaucho

His machete spoke incessantly. He wove a grill-work of strokes around his scarlet body. His head looked like a raw meat-ball. His features were gone, drowned in his own crimson like the disk of the autumn sun.

He disappeared a moment, but still attempted another attack. They did not wait. Twenty edges bit into his flesh, a rifle pitched from behind the wall struck him on the head. . . .

Another blow. . . . A yell. . . . Then silence. . . .

And then, a command from the dark!

"Don't kill him!"

Under the trees, the colonel and his frowning officers examined the wounded man. A stub of tallow on the gun of the sentinel served as a torch. The light flickered jerkily over their faces. The prisoner, seated on a rock, bled trickle by trickle.

Naked from the belt up, his breast crisscrossed with eyelets in which the blood mixed with hair, he gasped and panted. A sword-cut looped his right shoulder. The blood brimmed over his eyebrows.

Matted locks patched his forehead. His left arm was a hash at the end of which his hand, sliced across, poured blood on the knee where it lay. From behind, his flanks rose sore as the haunch of a broken horse, and the bronze neck glistened in tangled hair. Stripes of soot wound around him like more slashes.

With no doctor nor first-aid material, they could hardly help him. Neither would he lie on the cloak that they offered. In a stupor kin to fear, they watched him die.

That man was the incarnate flesh of the insurrection; the ranges of hills hid such human cordilleras. He was indeed only one, and yet they shrank beside him. He was the victor, and his impregnable strength seemed to parade before death.

The reflection of the fire crowned a hill in the distance. A cloud rosy as the wing of a flamingo had risen to the zenith, and it deepened the night by contrast. Silence had followed on the clamour of flight. From the mists trailed a breath of baked earth.

Little by little, the sphinx before them overpowered the soldiers into admiration. The gaucho bled ceaselessly. He wallowed now in a puddle. The colonel, abashed by the anomalous situation of that frightful man who inspired at once rage and pity, voiced thoughts directed apparently to the night.

. . . "They don't know what they are doing. They crown chieftains who rob them and turn the authorities against them, and then they kill one another. . . . They don't stop to think that the arms of the King will triumph. . . ."

The man spit a red phlegm to one side.

". . . will triumph in the end," went on the colonel, "and there will be no quarter. . . ."

"Colonel, you goin' to shoot me now?" the wounded man interrupted.

The soldiers looked at each other out of the corners of their eyes, and the officer, as if he had not noticed, questioned the rebel:

"How many were you?"

"Five. Look, I was goin' on the trail to my ranch, see? And I pick up the tracks. Here goes Spain, I says to myself. They went by just awhile ago. And I trailed too. I bumped into four boys, friends of mine, and they come along. Then it was night. We couldn't see. . . . We made the tracks by the smell of the manure. I thought it was ten. . . . And when I saw it was some more, I didn't want to go back. . . ."

Some more, meant over a hundred; but the man's arithmetic was limited by his thumbs.

"I got such an itch to fight! . . . You go on with the mules, I says to the others. I'll stay to watch the bonfire and I'll tell you about it. I took off my shirt and packed it away. That's the way with us poor, colonel. The hide heals; but the rag . . ."

He spit again, picking his nose with the fingers of his remaining hand, while he related his plot.

"Well, we waited on our bellies in the grass till the moon went down. And all of a sudden . . . bing! We put the match to the field. . . . You finish the story, colonel!"

Muddy laughter burst from his bloody face into the colonel's. His pride in that heroic prank made him so ugly that the officer shuddered.

"Then, by yourself . . ."

"Just me, colonel."

Death of a Gaucho

"Don't lie to me!"

The red threads that streamed on his forehead became two tiny cascades; his ribs caved, and without answering he slumped down, muttering through blood a *viva la patria*.

No one looked up. The prisoner shuffled his feet, and bloody filth bubbled between his toes. Now he was nauseated, and little shivers chattered his teeth. The officer, hardly noticing that now he no longer addressed the gaucho with the familiar pronoun, reproached him:

"What do you know of a *patria?*"

The wounded man looked at him silently. He stretched an arm to the horizon, and the mountains lay under his finger—the fields—the rivers—the nation that the guerrillas bulwarked with their breasts—the sea perhaps—a piece of the night. . . . The finger was lifted still higher, and remained so, straight to a star. . . .

The eyes of the watchers grew shadowed. Beards dipped in the collars of their capes.

And the silence rose and swelled, almost to anguish. The improvised torch burned low.

A swarm of ideas spun in the head of the officer, and he half-closed his eyes. That *patria* with its violent fatality forced itself upon him. In the name of what, did it stir such courage? The lives of these men were breathed out before it like funeral incense, and the secular idols were powerless:— God, Spain, the King. . . .

At that moment one of the officers approached softly.

"Colonel . . ."

The chief started.

". . . he seems to be dead . . ." the officer concluded.

And he snuffed out the tallow stub.

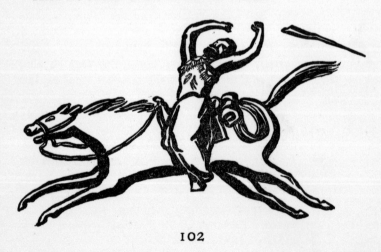

3. HOLIDAY IN BUENOS AIRES

Lucio V. Lopez

After the War of Emancipation, Argentina was plunged in civil conflict. There were two great factions: the *unitarios* who desired a strong aristocratic government in the capital, ruling the provinces as they had been ruled under the Spanish viceroy; and the *federales*, represented by the humbler provincials and gauchos, who fought for a loose confederation with preponderance of local rights. The civil war ended with the dictatorship of Rosas who, ironically, although a Federalist, established in Buenos Aires a more strictly unitary rule than the *unitarios* had called for. When he had done their unifying work for them, Rosas was overthrown and succeeded by his great enemies—among them, Mitre and Sarmiento—Unitarians and aristocrats. It is only in the last generation with the economic progress of the provinces and the influx of immigrants, that the Argentine provinces have destroyed the rule of the wealthy estancieros whose headquarters are in Buenos Aires. President Hipólito Irigoyen is the leader of this bloodless economic and political revolution.

The author of this chapter, like most writers of 19th century Argentina, wielded the pen chiefly as publicist and political polemist. *La Gran Aldea*, from which this fragment is taken, is a quiet yet strong and savoury picture of the big town in the 1860's, before the task of fusing pampa, mountain and capital into one organism, had been completed. *La Gran Aldea* first appeared in a newspaper in 1882.

Holiday in Buenos Aires

O<small>H</small>, my childhood! My childhood was dreary and sad as those stretches of African sands that travellers gaze on for hours, as their ships approach the coasts of Senegal. When I was twelve years old I was taken, and with good cause, for an imbecile; I could not read except letter for letter awkwardly; and the lines clouded my eyes, while when I tried to form the words I felt my tongue bound cruelly, which made me stammer before others and feel the deep, poisonous wound of ridicule. I wrote clumsily, a wayward, barbaric hand. Oh, my copy-books! What pains they cost me, and how badly they came out!

Tales from the Argentine

My Aunt Medea had not troubled to have me taught anything. Why need I learn! Doctor Trevexo had already told her: "To occupy high positions in this country, it is not necessary to learn anything." And he was right. I was preparing myself for high positions, by following his advice to the letter.

My Uncle Ramón was not satisfied, however, with that system of spontaneous education, and the poor man, in the midst of all his amorous prowlings, would spend a few moments on me; he had taught me my alphabet in the headlines of dailies, and under his guidance I had learned to make my first scrawls.

I lived in the back of the house among the servants and their company enchanted me. I would be graceless indeed if I did not recall with affection those good people with whom I passed my first years.

The war between Buenos Aires and the Federalists had broken out again, and though I do not intend to devote many pages to politics, I must relate the part I took in the military fervor of those days.

Holiday in Buenos Aires

I have already given some idea of my aunt's excitement; she was on the side of war, with all her soul and in all good faith, believing herself a Greek matron, daughter of the invincible Buenos Aires, of the Athens of the River Plata, and of I don't know what all.

The battle of Pavón had taken place on September 17th, 1861, and the victory produced in Buenos Aires an indescribable wave of enthusiasm.

But before this encounter, my imagination was already gripped by the tales of the servants at home and by the lively after-dinner conversations between my aunt and her friends. I thought of nothing but soldiers and battles; I had a certain native talent for drawing, and I spent the evenings making pictures of the Buenos Aires army and fleet advancing on Urquiza; and among the ranks of soldiers, on a horse drawn with the most respectful care, I outlined the figure of my general, idol of my childish dreams, a kind of Cid in my mind, involuntarily caricatured by my unskilled pencil, he whom Providence had chosen to smash Urquiza, whom I pictured dressed like an Indian, with feathers in his hair, arrows, and a great knife at his belt, surrounded by the savage tribe which constituted his army.

On the night we heard of the battle, my aunt took me out for a walk to "get tongues," as she said.

The streets were jammed with people. Rumours of the great news were already afloat. A few refugees had arrived from the scene, and some proclaimed victory positively, others doubted, and the calmest wavered.

Buenos Aires then was not what it is today. The countenances of the two main streets, Peru and Victoria, have changed greatly in the twenty-two years that have passed: the *center* began at Calle Piedad and ended at Potosí, where the south vanguard of the shops was represented by the establishment of Señor Bolar, on the corner; a democratic counter at sunrise, when cooks and early housewives went to market, and bourgeois, even aristocratic, between seven at night and the curfew. The fashionable shopping district extended from Victoria Street to Esmeralda, and those five blocks were then the *boulevard de façon* of the metropolis.

Nowadays the hybrid and puny European shops,

totally lacking in local character, have exiled the urban store of that period, with its long counter and its formal white cat couched on it like a sphinx. Oh, what stores! I can see their entrances—no showcases, but tapestried with percales which hung on the walls, two and three meters out into the street; and among the percales, shining pieces of China silk, also nailed to the wall, and ready for any shrewd customer who could gauge quality between finger and thumb without having to set foot in the store.

That was commercial good faith, and not like now, when the enormous showcases feast the eye but make no attempt to provide the touch with its indisputable rights which our mothers demanded.

And what clerks! What salesmen, those of the stores then! How far indeed are the French and Spanish storekeepers of today from possessing the lineage, the social virtues, of that gilded youth, native born, last descendants of the aristocratic retailers that were colonial. No girl or lady went down the street without stopping to speak most cordially to the comfortable groups in chairs outside, presided over by the owner of the establishment. And when the lovely shoppers entered a store, the owner left his friends, greeted his customers with an effusive handshake, asked the mother after *that gentleman*, paid the daughters polite little compliments, took the *mate* from the hands of the shop-boy and tendered it with exquisite courtesy to the ladies; and only after having fulfilled all the requirements of this preface to gallantry, did customers and salesmen turn to the arduous affair of business.

Those stores smelled ineradicably of English wool, because there were always four or six great rolls of stuff near the door, and these, the solid merchandise, at the same time served usefully as seats for the frequenters of the establishment. Also, the counters were spread with rugs which displayed a whole printed zoo, tigers, panthers, pumas and ruddy lions, reposing majestically on historical woollen landscapes which the Manchester factories substituted for the Aubussons and Gobelins we then lacked.

How agile the owner, as with one hand on the counter he leaped to the other side! How gracefully he unfurled, at one stroke, as if with sleight of hand, the piece of percale, muslin or *barège*, wrapped around the board that, bared of its precious merchandise, was abandoned indifferently on the counter. What flexibility of movement, what dispatch the shop-keeper of those days displayed when he measured the bought yards on his stick, and with elegant carelessness let them billow high on the counter, while he caressed the fabric between his fingers, carried it nearer the eyes of the customer, put it in her hand, rubbed it to prove its innocence of starch or other factory artifice, and even brought the only glass in the store full of water and dipped one end of the muslin into it, to establish its absolutely fast dye.

No customer could withstand the charm, the skill, the convincing spells of those sorcerers.

But these shop-keepers were the dandies; there were also the sirens, so called because their bodies were divided by the line of the counter like those of the enchanting wraiths of the sea by the line of the waves.

The siren shop-keeper was a human being from

head to abdomen, and fish from abdomen to feet.
Correct the upper façade, with all the elegance that
could be desired; from the other side of the counter, the customer saw nothing, but the siren could
not leave his counter safely, because, as this was his
element, if he abandoned it, he displayed perforce
an indecorous tail; the siren shop-keeper wore a
swallow-tailed coat to economize on trousers, and
slippers to avoid the discomfort of shoes; so that the
counter concealed the least beautiful, but by no
means the least interesting, part of the statue.

Of the princes of the metropolitan counter, the
most famed was beyond a doubt Don Narciso
Bringas: a great merchant, a great patriot, born in
the neighborhood of San Telmo, but adopted by
Peru Street as king of the counter. There was no
counter to compare with his: all the other owners
together could not have spread a piece of percale and
furled it again like Don Narciso and if the pyramid
itself had questioned his love of Buenos Aires,
against the pyramid itself he would have fought
for that right.

I recall him so vividly, that if I were an artist

Holiday in Buenos Aires

I could paint his portrait from memory and with my eyes closed: stubby, short-legged, mobile as a squirrel, with a large head, long curly hair and a wide, ample forehead that revealed all his talents. His hands were like wings, his eyes were fireflies; his dulcet, ingratiating voice attracted sympathetically and he possessed a vocabulary that Molière himself would have envied, to bestow upon his learned ladies.

A great patriot, Don Narciso had taken part in the revolution of September and in Cepeda, the events of which he related night after night, explaining the most remote causes of the disaster with convincing reasons. But, if in the middle of the tale some lady of high society, and above all of high politics, entered the store, Don Narciso left his guests, leaped the counter and lined up the salesmen from chief to shop-boy, and then began the battle of calicos with a series of strategic maneuvers which unfailingly brought him victory, by a combination of processes as logical as Napoleon employed.

When I had come to know him well, I realized

what a worthy person he was. One of his multiple talents was the ability to attune himself to the circumstances of the customer, precisely as a violin is keyed to the note given by the conductor of an orchestra. Don Narciso raised or dropped his tone according to the social hierarchy of the person with whom he was dealing: he mastered the entire scale; possessed all the nuances of the cultured speech of the time, and sang high C to the lady while he struck an octave below for her cook.

His attitude varied according to hour and person. In the morning he boldly used familiar terms to the half-breed or the creole who entered his store on her way back from market. If the customer was a native daughter of the land, he addressed her blandly as such: daughter this and daughter that. If he observed her to be Basque, French, Italian, foreign, in short, he bargained, mentioned the last price, spoke of giving at cost price, and began his sentences with *madamita*.* Oh! That *madamita*, emitted between seven and eight in the morning,

---

* *Madamita*. Literally, "little madame." Idiomatic use of the term, implying familiarity with the person toward whom it is used.

with the few words of imitation French that he knew how to babble, proved irresistible.

During the day he varied between daughter and little daughter, between the familiar and the respectful *you*, between *madame* and *madamita*, according to the age of the *gringa*, as he called the customer if she was not caught in his net.

At these hours, Don Narciso's *toilette* was careless; but at four sharp, and just as the Spaniard brought in the main meal of the day, Don Narciso dived into the profound regions back of the store, took a piece of Spanish castile soap out of an inside counter, washed himself with it in a crippled iron basin of satyr feet, and in the light of a stub of tallow candle, smoothed down the neck and bosom of his shirt to remove the limpness acquired during the day's labours, seized his unevenly toothed comb and arranged his curls without other pomade than a little quince gum prepared by himself for private use.

Thus embellished, he choked the then very fashionable high collar around his neck, and added a necktie of the national colours; ate in a trice, fed his clerks, and within five minutes was majestically ensconced in his throne at the forward end of the counter, glorious battlefield, where, leaning back with all the elegance at his command, he passed the sterile hours of sundown till night came, and the high-life of that period sauntered in to squabble over the novelties of the Bringas place.

My Aunt Medea was a leader there, and had the gossipy habit, common to certain ladies, of sharing with the storekeeper all the news of the day.

That night the conversations were all politics, and only we who have lived in the fervid air of Buenos Aires of that period, can appreciate the importance of the discussions around the counters in Peru and Victoria streets, and the accord in political and social outlook between Don Narciso Bringas and my Aunt Medea.

Naturally, therefore, my aunt that night went to the Bringas place.

"Viva la patria!" Don Narciso exclaimed as we entered.

"Viva!" replied my aunt. "I suppose you announce our triumph, Don Narciso."

"The most complete triumph, *señora*; Urquiza

has been completely routed, and all his army is dead or prisoners; the national guard of Buenos Aires has battled spotlessly. I myself sold two hundred pairs of stripes."

"A whaling-boat that just came from Zárate, brought the news that Urquiza has been taken prisoner," one of the people in the store added.

"Is it possible?" my aunt exclaimed.

"Yes, indeed, señora, not a doubt of it; why the youngsters that went in that army were just my cream."

At that moment we heard firecrackers exploding near by.

"Firecrackers!" Don Narciso exclaimed. "Bulletin, that's a bulletin! Caparrosa," he said, turning to the errand-boy, "go buy the bulletin in a jump, and come back flying."

The boy, who was behind the counter, leaped like a fawn, rose over the barrier and fled down the street toward the printer's, where the firecrackers continued to explode ceaselessly.

My aunt seated herself in the Bringas place to wait for the desired bulletin, and as the boy delayed,

Don Narciso sent another clerk and after him went three or four citizens too impatient to wait for the news. My aunt, who was not a woman to wait, also went out toward the corner, dragging me with her.

The mob jostled in front of an old house on the north side of Victoria Street, between Bolívar and Peru, and now and then a firecracker rose from the house itself and rent the skies.

My aunt pushed a way for herself, making unprecedented efforts to keep her shawl around her shoulders. On a table in the door of the shop, stood a young man about twenty-two years old, distributing with two or three other men the freshly printed news bulletin, and answering questions vivaciously in a thin whining voice which he vainly tried to make more virile.

Whenever anyone succeeded in obtaining his bulletin, he dashed away, after a struggle to break through the human wall that dammed the street.

My aunt waded deeper and deeper into the tightly packed mob. Caparrosa, the errand-boy from

Bringas', a nimble, lively little Gallego,* had managed to clamber up a railing, and almost in line at a tangent with the youth who was selling the bulletins, shouted to him:

"To me, Don Jacinto, to me; Don Narciso sent me. Eh, Don Jacinto, eh! Don Jacinto, Don Jacinto, I'm the errand-boy from Bringas'. One for me, here's the money"—and he displayed a bill crumpled to a wad in his fingers.

The youth, after a long time, and deafened probably by the cries of Caparrosa, saw him at last perched in the window and barely nodding into the door, rolled up the bulletin and yelled:

"Come across with the money!"

"There it goes, Don Jacinto, there it goes, grab it, there it goes," and Caparrosa pitched his money so skilfully that Don Jacinto caught it in the air, precisely as a cat snatches a fly.

Caparrosa took the bulletin and was about to drop himself from the window; but my aunt, who had already wedged a breach and taken a position, cried to him:

* A native of Galicia, a province of Spain.

119

"Don't come down, boy, don't come down, buy me another, wait——." Meanwhile she forced her purse which stubbornly would not open, until, after much pulling, she fished a *peso* and stretching her right arm as far as it could go, handed the money to Caparrosa, who still hung in the window.

"Another, Don Jacinto, another bulletin for Señora de Berrotarán: Psst, psst, Don Jacinto! Another bulletin!" he kept yelling, waving the only free hand that his enviable position in the window left him.

"Come across with the money," Don Jacinto again answered.

"There it goes, there it goes, grab it——" and Caparrosa again pitched the money, and Don Jacinto again caught it on the fly.

Caparrosa finally dropped off the railing with his bulletins, and together with him my aunt and I began pushing to get through the crowd.

Within a few minutes my aunt emerged, bathed in the perspiration of that battle; and settling her bonnet on her puffs, entered the Bringas place victoriously with the bulletin in her hand.

"Complete triumph! Here it is, look at it, read it!"

Don Narciso took the bulletin, my aunt seated herself in a chair and the others gathered around the reader. Don Narciso read in a moved voice. At the name of each warrior, cries of joy from the audience interrupted him.

Suddenly, Don Narciso's forehead clouds, he looks at my aunt, and at the others, raises his eyes to heaven, and with the most pitiful groan in the world exclaims:

"The *Conde Romano*, dead!"

"The Conde? What have you read? It cannot be! You must have made a mistake," my aunt cried in deep distress.

"Yes, señora, read it, see: 'We lament on our side, the death of the young man, the Conde Romano . . .'"

"Oh, what a pity! what a sorrow, what pain! More than one girl is going to die of grief: Joaquinita, for example, the Alegre girl, is madly in love with him; whenever she saw him pass by on horseback, all wrapped in his grey cape, that girl just couldn't control herself and she would go to the street-door to watch him. Poor child!"

"And the Vargas girl, Victorita, the same; she met him here one night and just couldn't take her eyes off him," Don Narciso said.

"And what of the enemy army?" one of the citizens said.

"It went to the devil, then; one doesn't ask."

"Give me my bulletin, Don Narciso; I am going home to give my husband the news, I am sure he doesn't know a word of what has happened."

"Very good night, Doña Medea. You know I have fine blue and white bunting, and crêpe of the national colours at your disposal for when the army returns. Of course you will be decorating the front of your house. . . ."

"Of course! I count on you and on all your store. . . . Ah! The death of the Conde doesn't permit me to enjoy the news absolutely."

"Come, come, Julio," and my aunt turned to go.

"And this boy is yours?" one of the visitors asked.

"No, señor, I have never had any children; this

boy is a nephew of my husband's, a son of Tomás, who died some time ago."

"What Tomás?" the man asked Don Narciso in a lower tone, so my aunt could not hear.

"Don Tomás Rolaz, brother of Don Ramón, that was in the treasury. . . . Don't you remember?"

"Ah! yes, he was very much in favor of Urquiza?"

"The same."

"Ah! Good-bye, little friend," the curious gentleman who wanted to know so much about me said, taking me by the arm and holding me though my aunt was already in the street. "Good-bye . . . he deserves four bullets like the father," he added, still on the threshold and frowning.

I slipped away and clasped my aunt's arm, carrying stamped in my mind the face of that gentleman, in whom I had unfortunately awakened so much hate and so much thirst for vengeance.

4. THE PRIVATE LIFE OF FACUNDO

Domingo Faustino Sarmiento

Sarmiento is commonly looked up to by his countrymen as their greatest citizen. He was born of an aristocratic provincial family in 1811. He left his profession of school master to fight in the civil war between the *unitarios* of Buenos Aires and the gaucho *federales* of the pampa; and when these latter triumphed under Rosas, Sarmiento had to flee to Chile. Here he composed the volume of which a chapter follows. Facundo, whom Sarmiento abhorred with the passion of a partisan, was a real *caudillo* of the Rosas stamp; but the author generalised and universalised the man, together with his epoch, so as to produce quite unconsciously a book that is almost the Iliad of his nation. With Rosas' downfall, Sarmiento returned, entered politics and eventually became president of the Republic. Previously he had been sent by Mitre as minister to Washington, and he was greatly influenced by American civilisation, particularly by the pedagogy of Horace Mann. From first to last, Sarmiento was primarily an educator in action. It is interesting to note that he is more popular in Argentina, than the nation's purely military and political heroes. Sarmiento died in 1888.

The Private Life of Facundo

"Moreover those traits belong to the original character of the human race. The man of nature who has not yet learned to restrain or disguise his passions, displays them in all their power, and yields to their impulses."

BETWEEN the cities of San Luis and San Juan, stretches an extensive plain, called the Travesia, a word which describes, in this case, want of water. That waste appears for the most part desolate and sad, and the traveller approaching it from the east never fails to fill his water-bags at the last cistern he passes. The Travesia once witnessed the following strange scene. A fight with knives, so common among our gauchos, had forced one to flee from San Luis to the Travesia on foot, with his riding gear on his shoulder, to escape the police. Two others were to join him as soon as they had stolen horses for the three.

Not only hunger and thirst threatened him in the desert, for a man-eating jaguar had been stalking the trails of all travellers for a year, and more than eight persons had already fallen prey to his awakened taste for human flesh. It sometimes happens that man, in those places where he disputes the supremacy in nature with beasts, becomes the victim of bloody claws; and when the jaguar begins to acquire the taste, and turns to this new chase, the chase of mankind, it is called a *cebado*, or man-eater. The sheriff nearest the region he raids assembles the best huntsmen in the neighborhood, and he leads the pursuit of the beast, which seldom escapes the law.

Our fugitive had walked some six miles when he thought he heard the distant roar of the beast, and he shuddered. The roar of a jaguar somewhat resembles that of a boar, but it is shriller, more prolonged, harsh, and though there may be no danger its sets the nerves quivering, as if the flesh in itself felt the menace of death.

The roar came clearer and nearer; the jaguar was on the trail, and there was only a small carob-tree in the distance. He must hurry, he must run, for the roars grew more frequent, and each was louder, deeper than the one before.

Finally, pitching his saddle to one side of the path, the gaucho made for the tree, and, though the trunk was weak, he climbed it and managed to lodge himself in its branches, half-hidden and swaying. From that post he could see the road, and he watched the great cat advancing rapidly, sniffing the earth and roaring more often as he sensed his prey near. The beast passes the place where the gaucho left the path, and loses the scent; thrashes about, infuriated, and then sees the saddle, which he rips at one blow, strewing bits in the air. Thus thwarted, more maddened, he hunts for the trail, picks it up, and raising his eyes sees his prey rocking the sapling under his weight, as if it were a reed and he a bird perched upon it.

The jaguar stopped roaring, bounded toward him,

and the great fore-paws struck on the slender trunk, two yards from the earth; the tree quivered convulsively, as if through the very nerves of the baffled gaucho. The beast attempted to spring upon him, failed, and circled the tree, measuring his height with inflamed and blood-thirsty eyes; and finally, roaring with rage, stretched himself out on the ground beating his tail ceaselessly, his eyes fixed on the man, his parched jaws hanging open.

This horrible scene had lasted two mortal hours; the forced posture of the gaucho and the fascination that held him to the bloody, immobile gaze of the jaguar, whose overpowering attraction he could not withstand, had begun to weaken him; he already felt upon him the moment he would drop exhausted into the wide jaws when the distant beat of galloping horses brought him a hope of rescue.

And indeed, his friends had seen the tracks of the jaguar and ran without hope of saving him. The scattered riding gear sent them flying to the scene, and to unwind their lassos and throw them over the brute, now choking and blind with rage, was the work of a second. The beast, caught between two ropes, did not escape repeated stabs from the piercing dagger of the man who was to be the victim, and now avenged himself for his prolonged anguish. "I knew then what fear could be!" General Juan Facundo Quiroga would say to his officers as he finished the tale.

They called him, too, the Tiger of the Plains, and the title was not inappropriate. Phrenology, or comparative anatomy, has suggested the relationships between the form and the moral tendencies of human beings, and some of the animals which they resemble. Facundo—for thus he was known for a long period in the provinces (General Don Juan Facundo Quiroga and His Excellency the Brigadier General Don Juan Facundo Quiroga, all this came afterwards, when society had taken him to its bosom and victory had crowned him with laurels) —Facundo, then, was short and heavy; his broad shoulders upheld on a stocky neck a well-formed head covered with very thick, black curly hair. His barely ovalled face was buried in this thicket which matched an equally dense, crisp and curly beard that rose to his cheek-bones, prominent enough to disclose a firm and tenacious will.

His black eyes, full of fire and shaded by bushy brows, brought involuntary terror to the man upon whom they were fixed, for Facundo never looked straight ahead; through habit, or artifice, or a wish to make himself fearful, he generally kept his face down and looked through his eyebrows, like the Ali-Baba of Montvoisin. The Cain portrayed by the famous Ravel theatrical company recalls Quiroga to me, but without the artistic positions, which do not fit him. For the rest, his features were regular, and the pale darkness of his skin went well with the shadowing beard.

The structure of his head revealed, however, under its jungle, the gifted character of a man born to rule. Quiroga possessed those natural qualities which made of the student of Brienne a hero of his country, and of the obscure mameluke who fought with the French at the Pyramids, the viceroy of Egypt. The society into which they are born gives these characters their particular mode of expres-

The Private Life of Facundo

sion; sublime, classical, so to speak, they lead civilized humanity in some places; terrible, bloodthirsty and wicked, they become elsewhere its stain and its hate.

Facundo Quiroga was the son of a humble native of San Juan, who, having settled near the Plains of La Rioja, had acquired a fair fortune in sheep. In 1779 Facundo was sent to his father's birthplace to receive the limited education that its schools afforded: reading and writing. When a man comes to be heralded for his deeds by the hundred trumpets of fame, curiosity or a spirit of investigation traces back through his insignificant childhood to link it into the biography of the hero, and not seldom, among fables invented by flattery, the germs of his characteristic traits are discovered.

It is related of Alcibiades that, when he played in the street, he would lie down in the road to defy a coachman who requested him to make way in order not to be run over; and of Napoleon, that he ruled over his school mates and entrenched himself in his room to resist an expected insult. Of Facundo several anecdotes are told today, a good number of which depict him completely.

In his boarding house he could never be persuaded to sit at the common table; in school he was haughty, wild and solitary; he never mingled with the other children except to head rebellion or to beat them. The master, weary of struggling with that untameable character, procures a stiff, new lash which he displays to the frightened children: "This," he says, "will be tested on Facundo!" Facundo, then eleven years old, hears the threat and on the next day measures it. He does not know his lesson, but he asks the master to listen to it himself, because the assistant dislikes him. The master assents; Facundo makes one mistake, two, three, four; then the master uses the lash, and Facundo, who has calculated it all, even to the weakness of the chair in which the master is seated, gives him a buffet, overturns him, and in the resulting confusion escapes to the street and hides in a vineyard, from which he is not extracted till three days later. Is not this already the chieftain who will defy all society?

The Private Life of Facundo

When he reaches adolescence his character becomes more marked. He grows more sombre and more savage; a passion for gambling, that lust of rude souls who need a powerful stimulus to rouse them from the sluggishness in which they drowse, completely possesses him at the age of fifteen. Because of that, he acquires a reputation in the city; because of that he becomes intolerable in his boarding-house; because of it too, he finally shoots at one Jorge Peña, spilling the first drops of the torrent of blood which is to break his way through the world.

From the time he reaches maturity the strand of his life is lost in a labyrinth of fights and flights in the neighboring towns; sometimes hidden, pursued always, gambling, working as a peon, he dominates everything that approaches him, and deals out dagger-thrusts. Today at the Godoy Estancio in San Juan they point out adobe walls built by Quiroga. There are some in the regions of La Rioja, in Fiambalá. He showed others in Mendoza, at the very place where one afternoon he had twenty-six officers who had been taken prisoners at Chacón dragged from their homes and executed, to appease the spirit of Villafañe; during the campaign of Buenos Aires he also disclosed some of his work as a wandering peon. What brought that man, reared in a decent household, son of a prosperous and honest father, to a hireling's position, and moreover made him choose the dullest, crudest kind of labor, which requires only physical strength and endurance? Was it because the adobe worker receives double pay and by hurrying can acquire a little money?

The most connected account I have been able to obtain of this obscure and wandering period of his life is the following:

Towards 1806, he went to Chile with a consignment of grain, on his father's account. This he gambled away, as well as the pack-animals which had brought it, and the family slaves who had accompanied him. He often drove herds of stock to San Juan and Mendoza for his father, and these always met the same fate; for with Facundo, gambling was a fierce, burning passion, which consumed his heart. This constant loss of possessions must at last have wearied the paternal generosity, because in the end their friendly relations were cut short.

When he had already become the terror of the Republic, one of his followers asked him, "General, what was the largest bet you ever made in your life?"

"Seventy pesos," Quiroga answered indifferently, though he had just won two hundred at a single throw. He explained that in his youth, he had once bet seventy pesos, all he had, on one card, and had lost.

But this fact has its symbolic meaning. He had been working for a year as a peon on the ranch of a lady, in Plumerillo. Facundo distinguished himself for his promptness in going to work, and for the influence and authority he exercised on the other laborers. When they wanted a holiday to get drunk on, they spoke to Facundo, who told the lady, promising to have them all back at work on the following day, and he never broke his word. For such intercession, the peons called him *the father*.

At the end of the year's steady work, Facundo asked for his wages, which came to seventy pesos. He mounted his horse and set out without knowing where he was bound; saw a number of people in a store, alighted, and handing his seventy pesos over the heads of the group which surrounded the dealer, bet all his money on one card; lost, and again rode on in no special direction, when he was overtaken by a Judge Toledo, who stopped him to ask for his working papers.

Facundo brought his horse up as if to give them to him, pretended to search for something in his pocket, and laid out the judge with one thrust of his dagger. Was this a revenge for his loss? Or a sop to the hate for civil authority of a gaucho outlaw, or was he merely adding a new deed to his rising fame? Both. These revenges on the first being that he encountered occur frequently in his life. When he was addressed as General and had colonels under his command, he had one of them given two hundred lashes at his house in San Juan for having, he said, cheated at cards; to a young man, another two hundred for taking the liberty of joking when Facundo was in no such mood; and to a woman in Mendoza, two hundred lashes for daring to call, "Good-bye, General," when he passed in a rage because he had not succeeded in frightening a neighbor of his, who was peaceful and judicious as well as a brave gaucho.

Facundo reappears later in Buenos Aires, where in 1810 he enrolls as a private in the *Arribeños*, a regiment commanded by General Ocampo, a native of his own province, and afterwards president of Charcas. The glory of a military career lay before him in the sun of early May; and no doubt his unflinching temperament, and his instincts for destruction and butchery, reformed by discipline and ennobled by the sublime goal of the struggle, would have returned him one day from Perú, Chile or Bolivia, another of those generals of the Argentine Republic who like many brave gauchos rose from the ranks. But Quiroga's rebellious spirit could not endure the yoke of discipline, the order of the barracks, or the delay of promotion. He felt himself destined to rule, to rise at one bound, to forge for himself, in spite of civilized society or against it, a career of his own, combining courage and crime, discipline and chaos. Later he was recruited for the army of the Andes, and enrolled among the "mounted grenadiers" of San Martín. Lieutenant García made him his assistant, and very soon his desertion left a gap in those glorious ranks. Then Quiroga, like Rosas, like all the serpents who have flourished in the shelter of their country's laurels, became known for his hate of the soldiers of Independence, whom both Quiroga and Rosas have slaughtered so horribly.

Deserting in Buenos Aires, Facundo sets out for the provinces with three companions. A squad overtakes him; he turns the encounter into a real battle, which hangs in the balance for a time, until, killing four or five, he resumes his journey, cutting a path to San Luis with his dagger through other squads sent out against him. He was to traverse this same road with a handful of men later, scattering armies instead of squads and arriving at the famous Citadel of Tucumán to wipe out the last traces of the Republic and civil order.

Facundo returns to his father's house in the plains. To this period belongs an episode which is well verified and which nobody doubts. Notwithstanding, one author whose manuscript I consulted, replied to my questions on the matter that he did not know that Quiroga ever attempted to extract money from his father by force; and I should like to adopt this view in the face of unvarying legend and against public opinion. The contrary would be horrible! The story goes that his father refused him the sum he demanded, and that Quiroga, when both his parents were taking their siesta, locked the door and set fire to the thatch roof which commonly covers houses in that region.

But it is certain that his father once requested authorities at La Rioja to arrest him in order to curb his excesses, and that Facundo, before his escape, went to La Rioja, where his father was at the time, and taking him by surprise gave him a buffet and said: "You wanted me arrested, did you? Take that, and now have me jailed!" and thereupon mounted his horse and galloped away. A year later he returned, threw himself at the feet of the old man, and the two sob together; between the father's protests and the son's assurances peace is re-established, though on a fragile and ephemeral base.

But his wild habits and character do not change;

racing, gambling, and rides in the plains are made scenes of more violence, more stabbings and constant assault, so that at last he becomes intolerable to all and his freedom is threatened.

It was then that a monstrous idea which he shamelessly spoke of gripped his mind. The deserter from the *Arribeños*, the "mounted grenadier" who refused immortality at Chacabuco and Maipú, determines to join the gang led by Ramirez, born of the similar Artigas * troop, whose renown for crime and for hatred of the cities which it harasses, had reached Los Llanos and filled the authorities with terror. Facundo departs to attach himself to those buccaneers of the pampas, and perhaps the knowledge of his nature and of the powerful re-enforcement he means to the outlaws leads his alarmed fellow-provincials to advise the authorities at San Luis, through which he will pass, of his infernal plan. Dupuy, then the Governor (1818), has him arrested, and he disappears for a time among the common criminals in jail.

* Artigas was the gaucho leader of the pampas of Uruguay; he fought against the central rule of Montevideo in the same spirit as Facundo against Buenos Aires.

The Private Life of Facundo

But this jail of San Luis was to be the first rung of the ladder on which he climbed to subsequent heights. General San Martín had sent a great number of Spanish officers of all ranks, taken prisoners in Chile, to San Luis. Driven perhaps by suffering and humiliation, or hoping to rejoin the Spanish armies, these prisoners mutinied one day and opened the cells of all the common criminals to add their assistance to the general attempt to escape. Facundo was one of these prisoners; but barely had he reached the door, than he raised the iron bar of his fetters and split the skull of the very Spaniard who had freed him, ploughed through the mutineers and left a path of corpses on the wide street. Some say that the weapon he used was a bayonet, and that he killed only three; but Quiroga himself speaks of the bar and mentions fourteen dead.

Perhaps this is one of those idealizations with which popular imagination poetically adorns its beloved strong men; it may be an Argentine version of the jawbone exploit of Samson the Hebrew Hercules; but Facundo looked upon it as a crown of glory. Whether with bar or bayonet, he man-

143

aged to put down the mutiny and thus to make his peace with society and to be granted his country's protection; so that his name flew everywhere ennobled and cleansed, though with blood, of the stain upon it. Covered with glory and his country's creditor, Facundo returns to La Rioja, with credentials of his behaviour, and displays to the gauchos of Los Llanos new titles which confirm the terror that his name has begun to inspire, because there is something imposing, something which conquers and rules, in a man rewarded for the murder of fourteen at once.

Here ends the private life of Quiroga, from which I have omitted a great number of episodes that depict only his savage nature, bad training, and the fierce and bloody instincts native to him. I have related only those that explain the temperament which, though it may take a different course, belongs none the less to the same type of chieftains who have finally managed to destroy urbane civilization—the type lately summed up in Rosas, the lawmaker of this barbarous order which has displayed to the full its hate of European culture through brutalities and atrocities as yet unmatched in history.

Something still remains to be told of the spirit and nature of this pillar of the Federation. A literate man and boyhood friend of Quiroga who has provided me with many of the facts I record, includes in reference to Facundo's early life the following curious remarks: That he did not steal before he became a public official, not even in his most pressing moments; that he not only enjoyed fighting, but even paid for that privilege and for the sake of insulting the bravest; that he intensely disliked decent folk; that he never drank; that he was extremely reserved when young, and that he wanted to inspire more than fear, terror, and made it known that he had sorcerers or was a diviner himself; that he treated his intimates like slaves; that he had never confessed, prayed nor heard mass; that when a general he was seen once at mass, and that he himself said that he believed in nothing. The naïveté of the statements is proof of their truth.

All the public life of Quiroga seems to me summed up in these facts. I see in them the great man, the genius in spite of himself, and unknown to himself a Cæsar, a Tamerlane, a Mahomet. He cannot be blamed for being born so; he will stoop to anything, to gain power, to rule, to fight city and police. He is offered a rank in the army and he scorns it, because he cannot wait to rise, because there is too much submission, too much harness on personal will, too many generals weigh upon him, a uniform binds his body and discipline lays out his steps; all this is intolerable! His life on horseback, a life of dangers and powerful emotions, has steeled his spirit and hardened his heart; he hates instinctively, ineradicably, the law which has persecuted him, the judges who have condemned him, all that society and order from which he has early detached himself and which looks upon him with suspicion and contempt. So that unconsciously he expresses the theme of this chapter: "The man of nature who has not yet learned to restrain or disguise his passions, displays them in all their power, and yields to their impulses." This is human nature, and thus it is found in the pampas of the Argentine Republic. Facundo is a type of the primitive savage. He knew no authority; his rage was that of a wild beast; his matted and blackened mane fell over his eyes in clumps, like the serpents on the face of Medusa. He roared hoarsely and his eyes glinted like daggers.

In a fit of passion he picked out the brains of a man with whom he quarreled at cards; he tore both ears off his mistress because she once asked him for thirty pesos to pay for a wedding ceremony to which he had agreed; he split the head of his son Juan with an axe, because he could not quiet him otherwise; and beat a beautiful señorita in Tucumán whom he was unable to seduce or rape. He behaved entirely like a man still brute, but not therefore stupid or completely without ideals. Incapable of earning admiration or esteem, he wanted to be feared; but this desire possessed him so completely that it determined all his behaviour, and he spent his life producing terror of himself, in the towns as well as in the soldiers, in the victim about to be executed as well as in his wife and children. Incapable too of holding the reins of democracy, he substituted terror for patriotic service; ignorant, he surrounded himself with mystery and made himself impenetrable, and by means of a natural shrewdness, an unusual gift of observation and the credulity of the mob, pretended to foresee events, so that he acquired great prestige and renown among the people.

Quiroga is remembered in the provinces by an inexhaustible store of anecdotes; his sayings, his decisions, have an individual stamp that give him something of an oriental air, a certain Solomonic cast in the popular mind. And indeed, is there much difference between the famous judgment of cutting the child in half to decide who was the mother, and the following method of discovering a thief?

Something had been stolen by a soldier, and all efforts to find the thief had failed. Quiroga lines up the troop, orders a number of rods cut, all the same size, one for each man and has them distributed; then, he states very positively: "The man whose rod is the longest tomorrow, is the thief." On the following day the troop is again lined up, and Quiroga proceeds to compare the rods. One soldier is found to have a rod shorter than the others. "Scoundrel!" shouts Quiroga. "You're the one . . ." And he was indeed; his confusion betrayed him. The method was simple: the credulous gaucho, fearing that his rod would really grow, had cut off a piece. But only a superior man who knew something about human nature would have used it.

Again, some riding gear had been stolen from a soldier, and the thief could not be found. Facundo orders the troop to march before him, and watches, his arms crossed, his eyes searching. He has already announced: "I know who it is," with irrefutable conviction. They file by, many pass, and Quiroga does not move; he is the statue of Jupiter, the image of a God on the Day of Judgment. Suddenly, he throws himself on a soldier, and says sharply: "Where is the saddle?"

"Over there, señor," the man answers, pointing to a thicket.

"Four sharpshooters," Quiroga shouts. What revelation was this? That of crime and terror to a shrewd man.

Once a gaucho was defending himself from a charge of theft; Facundo interrupted him thus: "This rogue has begun to lie; now then . . . one

hundred lashes!" When the prisoner was sent out,
Quiroga turned to a man who had witnessed the
scene, and said: "Look, boss; when a gaucho is talking and begins to trace designs on the ground with
his foot, it's a sure sign he is lying." After the
lashes, the gaucho retold his story more accurately,

which was, that he had made away with a yoke of
oxen.

Facundo at one time required and called for a
man of daring and determination to send on a dan-
gerous errand. He went on writing when the man
was brought before him, raised his eyes after he had
been announced several times, gave him one look
and turning back to his work, said: "Eh! . . . He

is good for nothing. I asked for a brave and fearless man!" It was then discovered that the man was in fact a fool.

There are many such episodes in the life of Facundo. And while they reveal a superior man, they have established for him a mysterious reputation among rude folk who went so far as to credit him with supernatural powers.

5. THE DEVIL IN PAGO CHICO

Roberto J. Payró

The versatility of Payró is suggested by this tale
so distinct in tone and method from *Laucha's Marriage*. Payró was a journalist, who wrote pro-
fusely in all forms, from the theater to the historical essay. His work lacks the conscious artistry
of the later generation; but its power is as fluent
and fertile as one of the great rivers that flow into
La Plata. Practically all the writers represented
in this volume were journalists. The journalism
of the Argentine Republic has ever been integrally
joined with the nation's evolution in politics and
the arts. Literature and action are not separate in
this southern nation, which explains perhaps why it
gives promise of so high a future.

This tale is from a volume called *Pago Chico*
first published in book form in 1908. The col-
lection of stories describes the life of a typical
farming community in the Province of Buenos
Aires—ranches and village. The word *Pago* is
an untranslatable localism, meaning both *place*
and the intimate communal life of the place.
Chico means *small*.

The Devil in Pago Chico

VIACABA, that well-known gruff, hard-working and good settler, at one time had his dwelling some leagues from Pago Chico. It stood by the pool of a small arroyo which mirrored the cliff, steep and bare of vegetation, the puny willows and the corral that sheltered a scant herd of sheep; then turned almost at right angles back to its old bed and ran, leisurely, shallow, and turbid, into the meager stream of the Rio Chico, really never a river, even thus reënforced, except in times of a great rise, or a flood. Viacaba had lived there many years with his wife Panchita, his two sons Pancho and Joaquin, men already, Isabel, his daughter, a homely but intelligent little brunette, and a couple of peons, Santiago and Matilde, who, with the help of the old man and the two sons, were enough and to spare for the daily chores of the little ranch.

These chores were far from exhausting, though Viacaba owned many cows and some mares, and a few hundred head of sheep for his own use, not being much inclined to that branch of breeding.

The dwelling was ample, with several rooms. It could be seen from a distance, on its mound which was cut in two by the arroyo which, wilfully and capriciously, had not taken the easiest way, though there was plenty of level ground to run on. Perhaps, when its bed was laid, those lands formed an entirely different topography.

And just as the house could be seen at a distance, so from it the eye swept a vast horizon, curved, desert, completely level, a stretch of pampa covered with dry, bleak weed, grayish yellow; a dusty mat on which, as if deliberately traced, the wriggling greenish line of the arroyo banks made a band like new velvet galloon on a worn cloak.

The Devil in Pago Chico

It was sultry just after noon that day. The plain quivered as if made of slight and vibrant sheets of steel, and dizzied with its blinding flashes. The sky was almost white, absolutely cloudless, but into it floated great, invisible rolls of vapour breathed off by the heat. Strident crickets whirred incessantly, and the air carried a monotonous buzz of insects, coming from no definite place, but deafening, stupefyingly persistent.

It is not strange, that, fatigued by the morning's work, and overcome by the heat, the Viacaba household slept—the men on the porch that faced east, and the women indoors, where the dark gave a momentary freshness.

The suffocating air did not stir, this day like every other at this hour; for the drought was so prolonged and menacing that the animals had begun to ail and lose weight, sign of a probable epidemic. The sleeping men breathed laboriously, large drops of perspiration broke from their pores, sudden and crystalline, to run in strands along their dark skins. They slept intranquilly, troubled by the heat and the flies, which hummed, insistent, despite their instinc-

157

tive slaps. And they would have gone on sleeping, prostrate and torpid, had not a galloping horse paused at the gate; the furious barking of the dogs, who a moment before lay stretched in the shade with lolling tongues, aroused the ranch from its siesta.

Matilde, an enormous, uncouth peon from Santiago whose feminine name fitted about like "a pair of guns on a Christ," rose, grumbling, lazily, and in spite of the sun that cracked the earth, with dragging steps went to find out who was the untimely horseman. The rest, looking toward the gate, glimpsed a black pony, even more black with sweat and dust, panting like a pair of bellows and jerking head, ears, and tail to evade the cloud of flies that had settled upon it. The traveller had entered with Matilde, who preceded him to tell Viacaba.

"It's a Frenchy that wants some water," he said. "Shall I give it to him?"

"Of course! And have him come into the shade."

When the man reached the porch all the others

had risen, and Panchita and Isabel were stirring inside, roused by the voices.

"Good afternoon, friend. Come in and sit down. Give him a drink of good cold water, Serapio. After that if you like, you will take a *mate*. And how can you travel, friend, in this sun when not even the snakes crawl out of their holes?"

The Frenchman explained that he had urgent business to transact at the town that afternoon, so he could leave on the "galley" the following morning.

He was a tall, thin young man, reddish, and very pale of eye, with a narrow forehead and a long, colourless nose hooked like the beak of a bird of prey; there was something furtive about him, in spite of his sharp long face, and his exaggerated courtesy did not successfully erase the unfriendly impression he had made from the first moment on those simple and crude men. A repulsive air floated about him, as if given off by his person, and the five ranchers, so different in appearance and manner, looked on him with distrust.

Greedily he drank the water fresh from the well, and sat on a bench, enjoying the shade of the porch, with his back against the rough whitewashed wall, and blinking to keep from falling asleep. When Isabel, followed by her mother, appeared from the kitchen with the bitter *mate* she had just prepared, he rose stiffly, bowing and murmuring obsequious words to the "señoguita" and the "señoga."

He sipped, not without some air of distaste, the acrid beverage to which he was unaccustomed and unctuously returned it to the girl. She, as she passed toward the kitchen with a great rustling of starched skirts, signalled to Pancho a little grimace and a side-long glance that conveyed how much she too disliked the stranger. Her mother watched him surreptitiously. The men made efforts to maintain the flagging conversation.

His visit lasted over an hour. Matilde meanwhile watered the pony and tightened its cinch, as if thus to hasten the guest's departure.

While he pulled on a black cigarette which Viacaba offered, the Frenchman spoke of the drought and the poor state of the ranches. He had come far, and all the country he had traversed was similarly desolate: pastures dry as kindling, lakes without water, drinking-holes bare and hard as rock, arroyos so low that they could nearly all be crossed at a jump, the cattle like skeletons, the sheep ailing and with a worse mange than ever, the mares skin and bones.

"We're lucky we haven't got it so bad yet," Viacaba exclaimed with some satisfaction.

But he looked up suddenly, alarmed, when the stranger said that in many places he had seen great whirls of dust that the wind raised from the bare ground.

"The dust-storms!" he murmured with fear in his voice. "They seem on the way!"

And he sat profoundly thoughtful, recalling the catastrophe, not suffered for many years, but which at one time had borne down upon him sowing destruction and devastation, and leaving the immense pampa totally depopulated of animals, and itself even seemingly dead and buried under an ashen and mobile mantle of dust.

The cracked, sour voice of the stranger, full of

discordant tones, heightened the disagreeable, hostile impression he had made on them all.

With the sun already low the Frenchman· departed bowing and mouthing reiterated grateful phrases. Viacaba accompanied him to the gate and the rest of the household lined up on the porch to watch him depart. The pony, rested by now, trotted more briskly, and as he was about to break into a gallop the horseman heard a shout from the gate:

"Watch out for the fag!"

"Oui! oui!" he answered, not understanding.

A moment later Isabel, returning with the inexhaustible bitter *mate*, voiced the common thought:

"I don't like that man one bit!"

"He's nothing good, I'll bet," Matilde growled as he went to saddle.

"He seems half . . . lady-like," Pancho the most tolerant, after Viacaba, muttered.

And though they sat for a long time in silence, that visit must have continued to trouble them, because Serapio did not say whom he meant when he added:

The Devil in Pago Chico

"There he goes, by the bush."

A shape, indeed now hardly visible, of a man on a horse moved rapidly away and into a high hay-field that stretched distantly toward the Pago Chico.

"Lady-like you said!" Joaquin, who had brooded over these words, objected. "Well, to me, what he looks like is just a bird of ill omen, with that hoot-owl's beak sticking out on his face. . . . Just so he hasn't put a curse on *us*. . . ."

"That's enough of omens, Joaquin!" Viacaba exclaimed. "Those *gringos* manage to trot out some faces! . . . just fierce! But what of it! Are they witches for that?"

Although Viacaba was superstitious too, age and experience had modified to some extent this inclination.

The peons, followed by Joaquin, went out to the fields, westward, where lay most of the ranch. To the east, beyond the creek, there were only some mares and the small herd of bay stallions.

The two women, with Viacaba and Pancho, remained on the porch, with no impulse to move in the stifling air. The sun, reddening, neared the west.

At dusk, when the others returned, drawn by dinner-hour, the sky in the west was an immense crimson shawl reflected to the east in a diaphanous veil, crimson too. And in front of this veil a straight column of dust-like vapour rose from the hay-field, whirling upon itself.

"I should say! They're beginning already," Viacaba called, seeing it on his way to the kitchen.

How had that man of the open, born in the pampa, who was a confidant of all its secrets, been able to make a mistake? Did he see badly? Or had the terrible idea of the dust-storms, the obsession of such a calamity, paralyzed his brain?

It was not, indeed no, the cloud that a circular current lifts and twists in the air, like an oriental column, from the dried soil, to dance it capriciously here and yonder and then drop it quickly, dissolved, erased from the air like a nightmare. No. The column was fixed at one point and rose and swelled in the quiet, heated air gilded and reddened by the last glow of the sun.

The Devil in Pago Chico

And as the light sank, the waves of scarlet that trailed it flowed down with it, little by little, like water through a crack. Slight breezes, messengers of peace, quivered and multiplied, ushering in the night.

It was dark now and nevertheless the column could still be seen in the high grass, vaguely luminous, as if it were the very same pillar that had guided the Israelites in the desert.

Meanwhile the Viacaba family, now more animated and chatty, ate in the kitchen around the fire, for the breeze, though tepid still, aroused them from their languor as it grew stronger and flew more certain wings.

The conversation, stilled now and then, persisted on the theme of the Frenchman, event of the day. And no one had a good word for him.

"That screech-owl can go to the devil! I've never seen an uglier beast," Joaquin insisted, superstitiously. "And how he stared, with those washed-out eyes, and in spite of all of his voolevooing! . . . To me he looked like . . ."

"The Bad One, no?" Matilde interrupted. "And

to me too! They say he is like that, whitish, with light eyes and the beak of a parrot. I didn't notice his feet because he wore boots. . . . But I'll bet he had hoofs, and no less!"

Like an answer to these words, the anguished voice of Panchita, who had just gone to the well for water, sounded in the patio a cry of alarm and of terror:

"Fire! . . . Fire! . . . Fire in the hay! . . ."

"Didn't I say so!" Joaquin murmured, dashing outside with the rest.

The threatening column, rising, swelling, illumined with fitful flashes, became a giant trunk with a small, round, whitish crest; then, when the wind blew more violently, suddenly faded; immediately, in the greater shadow, it seemed that the tree had fallen flaming from end to end, because drawn from its original site a line appeared, spitting fire, coals and tiny wandering flames that were reflected in the mists overhanging them. Then at once the red, resplendent line along the earth spread farther; crossed an enormous space in the east, from where the wind came, as if trying to fill the entire horizon. From the house luminous flashes, orange and yellow, could be seen wandering in the field, contrasted against the black night and in harmony with the crimson line of the fire, while in the sky a reddish patch seemed to match the trail of disaster. And the wind shook the high, dry, rustling grasses merrily, gurgling and laughing like a child running off after a prank. Musical rustlings filled the air with indeterminate refrains. Near the house, looking out over the plain, Panchita and Isabel watched, frightened at the spectacle. The men, having saddled hurriedly, galloped toward the field straight to the most visible point of danger; but they were so shaken that they could not carry out a consecutive thought. . . .

The wind, tired of laughing, amused itself now, combining curious and devastating fire-works. It approached the flames, picked up clouds of smoke and sprays of sparks; wove the smoke around the near-by bushes, illumined by the fire, pretending to light them too, and scattered the sparks like a bouquet, or tied them into harvest bundles of golden stalks; then let them die down or drop on the pasture in a delicate, destructive shower. . . . Or at one breath it abruptly put out the immediate red line, and then, as if regretting this diversion, brought it to life again with another breath till it flamed and made even the sky burn. . . . Gusts as from a monster oven reached the women, breaths from a forge, a muffled roar as of distant volleys, and an acrid odor of scorched straw exhaled from the dense masses of smoke that rolled across the plain.

Slowly at a distance, rapidly in fact, the line of fire advanced, and seemed to curve in an arc whose center was the ranch; gradually it crawled nearer, as if closing upon a site it had previously and strategically chosen. The plain between the ranch and the fire was bright, enormous shadows raced and wavered upon it: the plump ones of the clumps of hay and the long ones of the horsemen who circled near the blaze.

A rumble, a tattoo of alarm broke suddenly into the throbbing silence, making the earth shake; it was the herd, fleeing in terror, hammering upon the ground which echoed the hoofs like a drum. A formless shadow, enveloped in clouds of dust, passed with a glimpse of haunches and tangled manes to the wind. . . . And the furious drumming died down, lost in the night. . . .

"The horses!" shrieked Isabel in a heart-rending voice, torn from her lethargy.

"Holy Virgin! And who knows if we shall ever see them again," the mother moaned.

In their wake, harsher sounds, confused and unreadable, filled the pampa and reached the women swept by the blazing wind, full of smoke and bearing ashes that still were hot. . . .

Viacaba, his sons and his peons had flown thinking to be in time to smother the fire. But closer, their hearts failed; the tall, matted hayfield, the sturdy, compact rows, the yellowing harvest that could hide an upright man, burned as far as the eye could reach, crackling, flaming, exploding like thousands of petards sent off by connecting fuses. Gusts as hot as the fire itself blew on them; and they gazed at each other, their faces in sweat and soot, their eyes aglitter. The horses, their ears laid almost horizontally toward the fire, gasped and tossed their heads and refused to advance.

A little nearer, and they were lost in smoke and sparks, they seemed to ride into clouds among flying stars. The acrid smoke blinded them, accustomed as they were to an open fire, and the fiery blasts forced them to turn their faces, hair and beard half-singed. . . . Over them the luminous chaff hung for an instant and then went on to scatter disaster, snatched by the wind. . . . They could hardly hear each other's shouts, in the roar of the crackling hay.

". . . Counter-fire!" Viacaba was heard to yell as he jumped from his horse. The rest of the sentence was lost in the blare. . . .

Behind the curtain that the great fire cast in front of them, the night grew black as never. The moonless sky seemed to drop, and drop, blacker as it came, till it touched the very fire itself, except that below, the thick red stars went out one after another, leaving that part of infinity sinister and vacant. The horizon had advanced to within a few steps, and they seemed on the brink of some measureless abyss. . . . The glare itself pushed forward on the furious wind that blew from the furnace. . . .

The Devil in Pago Chico

At Viacaba's cry, they all dismounted. A signal brought them together, and they heard this shout:

"Not here! It would be worse! At the edge of the hay! . . ."

They retreated a stretch, pulling the bridles of the quivering horses that turned their heads toward the fire, their eyes like coals, snorting and blowing, making sudden efforts to be free and escape.

Thus, surrounded by red Bengal lights, men and beasts reached the edge of the hayfield, where the shorter grass began, dry and wilted too. Serapio hobbled the horses and tied them to a clump, some distance away, then joined the others.

Viacaba and Pancho were quickly touching off the low grass, in a band a little over a yard wide, more or less parallel to the line of the fire. Joaquin and Matilde behind them let the grass burn well down, then beat it out with brooms of greener hay, till it too was flaming, or with the saddle-blankets, unmoistened, because the water was too far away. Serapio helped them.

In that furnace they seemed smelters at a river of

incandescent metal; they panted, they sweated; their black faces, flushed and shining, swelled, bloated, lost their features, and their eyes flashed, and streams of ink poured along their foreheads and cheeks.

Useless sacrifice! The fire laughed beforehand at the obstacle they intended, with a trench of space: laughed at them, conniving with the wind, whose wings carried its messengers and propagandists far past the men and their struggle.

And the drumming that frightened the women reached them like a distant tremolo of cymbals between the smacks of the fire. . . . Viacaba raised his head aghast and with bulging maddened eyes yelled:

"Serapio! Matilde! The hacienda! The hacienda!"

Realizing at last the enormity of the disaster, they abandoned the fires and raced panic-stricken toward their mounts.

The horses were gone. Goaded by terror, they had managed to root up the bushes, and snorting, frenzied, impeded by the hobbles, in great insane leaps, stumbling blindly, wavering, streaming sweat, they had fled west, to salvation.

The men managed to catch and mount them and broke into a run in different directions as if following a given plan. But they had none. . . . Where to take the herds, in case they were not already scattered and lost in the gloom of the pampa? Where find a safe shelter? Where save them from this tremendous raid?

The women, dazed with fright and grief, stood where they were, their eyes fixed on the fire which advanced, advanced each minute more rapidly and intensely, not only to the houses, but to the right, to the left, north and south, cutting them off from the world, and with an impassable line around them cutting them off from retreat. The rumble of triumph, the assault without bugles, could be heard closer, closer, like bursts of laughter and shouts of harsh, discordant voices. . . . The heat was so great that the two unhappy creatures felt any moment they would faint, and fall strangled. . . .

The fire reached the arroyo. . . . Hope leaped in their breasts a moment. . . . But the flames laughed at the slight ditch, spread for it beforehand, and floated wisps across it with the wind their accomplice. Once on the other side, the fire advanced till it licked the gate and then joyously raced west, leaving the night greater behind it, dropping it at the very feet of the women who gazed numbly at the winged stars of the fire, snuffed out one by one in the cavernous night created by it. . . .

Beyond, to the right, where the Southern Cross gleamed, the straw served also as flying bridge to the devastating invasion. The entire stream flamed in a second. And from the other side, from the high bushes of the yard, the wind snatched shoals of sparks and tossed them at the women. . . . Some even landed on the house and went out in the thatch, too weak to touch it off. . . . They, in their supreme anguish, did not perceive the new danger. And sparks and blazing chaff danced by, larger and larger. . . .

"Mama! Mama!"

A terrible cry from Isabel proclaimed the ultimate catastrophe: the central thatch blazed with great puffs of smoke in a ring a yard around.

"Water! Water!" the mother shrieked, shaken from her apathy.

Both ran to the horse trough, near the well; one filled a basin, another a jug; but they could not throw far enough.

"You bring the water," blurted the mother.

And somehow, anyhow, climbing on a bench, bruising hands and knees, hampered by her garments, she clambered to the roof screaming desperately, as if they could have heard:

"Viacaba! . . . Pancho! . . . Joaquin! . . ."

Isabel brought her jugs and basins of water, racing, panting, bathed in perspiration. She, feverishly, hardly knowing what she did, threw herself upon the roof, held out her shaking arms, pulled the water up mechanically, and went to fling it on the swelling fire. . . . And while they were engaged in this exhausting and slow task, the wind riddled the house with its incendiary arrows. . . . A moment later the roof blazed at every point. . . .

"Come down, mama! come down! You'll be roasted alive!"

The wretched woman came down at last. Merrily as a bonfire, the dwelling flamed at its four corners, lighting up the patio to the gate, with its dishevelled willows tossed by the wind, and to the corral in which the sheep turned, trampled, climbed over each other baaing piteously, trying to tear down the strong fence. . . . And that dreadful and formidable blaze spread, blotted out the other, now distant in the horizon.

Far away, the men saw that torch and returned one after the other, full of despair.

Nothing could be done. . . . At great risk, they barely managed to remove a few things from the great oven. . . . The beams crashed, the porch went, in the red flare there were only blackened walls. . . . The family sat on the ground, numbed by helplessness and by distress, which their laconic phrases voiced. The visit of the stranger returned to their minds, in diabolic, terrifying features.

"Oh, the gringo, the gringo! . . ."

"He alone brought us this calamity! . . ."

"He witched us, sure . . ."

"The scoundrel must certainly have pitched his fag in the hay! . . ."

The Devil in Pago Chico

"No, boss! he was the Bad One, he was the Fiend! . . . Sure as this is a cross! . . ."

And the superstition became corroborated fact when on the morrow, stripped of everything, they took refuge in Pago Chico, and were told that no Frenchman had come there.

Then from mouth to mouth the legend became history, although the commissary investigated and announced that a man answering the description had been in the neighboring village of Sauce that afternoon, and next morning had taken the boat. . . .

Dawn came bleak and sad upon the fields. Men and women, drawn closer by distress, made a single, still little group. What yesterday had been comfort and plenty now was misery. . . .

The pampa, with the first faint light, lay swathed in an immense funereal cloak, which stretched to the horizons,—and the wind, still brisk, raised soot in clouds and sheathed the folk in soft, impalpable ash. . . .

6. ROSAURA

Ricardo Güiraldes

Ricardo Güiraldes marks an epoch in Argentina's letters. His great novel, *Don Segundo Sombra,* is the story of an archaic gaucho rendered by the sensibility of a modern. The cycle that began with *Martin Fierro* in the seventies is rounded. The *argentinidad* (to use a word of Ricardo Rojas) of Güiraldes is not however intellectual, like that of the deliberately national poet, Leopoldo Lugones: it is a thing of texture, of accent—a report and creation of the senses rather than a message of the mind. The earlier writers *knew* they were Americans; Güiraldes *feels* he is American. And this distinction is the new note in South American letters. The exquisite techniques of Europe are being acclimatised to convey a world utterly remote from Europe. This is true of writers like Lugones, Güiraldes, Quiroga (to mention three who are represented in this volume) even as it is true of Mexican painters like Ribera, Angel and Orozco.

Rosaura, published in 1922, is above all an "experiment in prose." The life of the pampa, its amazing counterpoint of delicacy and potency, is revealed through a design of words and of wordrhythm. To render this little masterpiece in English was a task of re-creation, rather than of translation.

The latest work of Güiraldes discloses new adventures: his sensibilities, fine and sure as a steel probe, had begun to touch the mystic dimensions of American life. His death is a great loss.

Rosaura

For my sister, Lolita, in 1914.

I

LOBOS is a tranquil town, in the middle of the pampa.

An indifferent boredom drifts through its tree-fringed streets.

Few passersby sound on its pavements, steps telltale as hoof-beats, and except at the train-hour or during the summer promenades on the plaza, fresh with evening quiet, nothing stirs the sober siesta which a spinster conscience seems to impose on the town's friendliness.

Like all our towns, Lobos possesses a plaza whose

blunt brick enclosure, exposed by a recent sacrifice of old vines, stretches across from the Church, and daily flaunts an artificial sleekness renewed by the long and flexible nozzle of a hose.

The Church is colonial style, its great courtyard of red flags rimmed with a single zig-zag marble parquet. In front, the plaza between, is the police-station with its coat-of-arms and its chief in view, while his orderly takes the air to the count of *mates* prepared by an ex-felon policeman, who trades re-tail in pardons.

A two-story branch of the Banco de la Nación overlooks one of the corners of the square. On the second corner, counting by display, the gastronomic windows of the *Jardin* confectionery, known by residents familiarly as "the Basque's," spread out an invitation for the afternoon. And while on the third, the store smiles percaline brightness, on the fourth the pharmacy reminds that there are ills in this world.

Here is all the community needs: justice, money, clothing, self-indulgence, and ideals, in moderate doses.

Rosaura

The main artery of the town's life, one of the streets opening into the plaza, is called *Calle Real* and is cobblestoned. Ornate souvenirs of some Louis nth on its houses are tempered by massive old elms in danger of being felled by a progressive administration which might not consider them fine trees.

In a row, monopolizing the privilege of the pavement noisy under wheels and hoofs, stand the Hotel de Paris, the Club Social, the *Globo* jewelry, the clothing store, and the *Modelo* shoe-shop.

Five or six blocks from this center, the squares of monotonous colourless structures built adjoining are brightened here and there by a bush or a tree whose serene crown looks out over the dusty bricks of the walls, flat and angular as a house of cards. The façades begin to glow yellows, greens, and sky-blues, blotting-paper tones. Doors and windows are framed in deeper hues. Through the doorways a glimpse of vines is caught reflected in polished tile floors.

On the fringe, the grocery store, once the headquarters for the alley, sleeps deserted, despite the mildly domestic air lent by a sorry team of hacks (one grey, the other dappled) dozing harnessed to a spring-wagon.

Villas scatter the town into a vast horizon of ranches, to which summer visitors bring the only glitter of wealth in the district.

The soul of Lobos was simple and primitive as a red bloom. Lobos thought, loved, lived, in its own way. Then came the parallel infinities of swift rails, and the train, marching armoured to indifference from horizon to horizon, from stranger to stranger, brushed its passing plume over the settlement.

Lobos fell ill of that poison.

II

In a car of the National Railways that afternoon rode a young man dressed in European style, irreproachably: collar and tie, soft hat, and country-suit that, though worn, retained in the lining of an inner pocket the label and date of delivery from Poole. His legs were encased almost to the knee in boots impeccably curved. Beside him balanced a suit-case from a great London house, colorfully patched with stickers that recorded stays at fashionable hotels and beaches. His coat hung from the clumsy rack. And the thick-seamed gloves lay like a pair of amputated Indian hands on the dusty table in the middle of which a litre of water danced spherically within a round-bellied jug of long and pretentious neck.

The youth's clothing proclaimed an education abroad. His dark skin, evenly laid either side of a lean nose, his high cheek-bones and rigidly correct bearing, revealed Castilian descent; something silent and searching in his pupils told several generations of watchful pampa life; and the native zest of a new race braced his easy laughter.

The inspector called him Don Carlos when he asked for the tickets. His age might have been gauged roughly as somewhere between twenty-five and thirty. With leisure, he glanced through a daily, at the cattle-market quotations.

The cars jarred abruptly, the asthmatic gasps of the locomotive died down, a yellow lantern illegibly flashed past, the earth-level rose to a platform outlined by a row of banana trees; the train stopped in front of the lighted corridor of that station that shut out the night.

"LOBOS"

People descended, people ascended. The boiler hissed like a deflating balloon. The buzz of a bee-hive rose from the crowd: politicians out campaigning, fashionable youths in gray felts and light shoes, personages displaying their official personalities, sheiks with straw hats about to slide off their greasy foreheads and stickily pomaded skulls, coachmen waiting for fares, *peons* for mail or on errands, while like perfume-blossoms in the jungle, the exuberant girls of Lobos came and went, shyly discreet or laughing excessively, nervous—who knows why.

Three went, arm in arm, slowly: one in sky-blue, another in pink, another in yellow. Toward Carlos' window they glanced with such bold curiosity that he was annoyed, squared his shoulders, breathed high, and flushed aggressively and violently as a turkey. In defense he fixed his eyes upon one of them, thinking to intimidate, but instead the girl held that gaze as wood does a plug.

Rosaura

They passed. Two or three times they promenaded the station from end to end, walking with the careless ease of coquettes. Carlos, no longer offended, took the play and gazed after the swaying little figure retreating as if in anger, or bored with his eyes into the pupils that became penetrable and docile.

And she with surprise felt her eyes opened like that, as if they had been careless windows, and her body overcome by a strange wave of languor.

But it was all play and when the train jerked out after a blazon of whistle and bell, as the elegant youth half bowed, they laughed openly, correcting that rudeness with a bare and almost involuntary dip of the head to the shoulder.

The car passed quickly, striking from the station windows a vibrant echo.

III

Her name was Rosaura Torres and she was the daughter of old man Crescencio, owner of the wealthiest livery-stables in town, an estate which counted no less than five cabs drawn by horses splendid for work, God willing.

It was large, half a block, this place of brick and unwhitewashed clay.

The hallway, dining room, kitchen and bedrooms faced front. Inside they were backed by a porch from the eaves of which hung, like slim and long sensual boas, intricate vines embracing hungrily. A tiny orchard containing one flower-tree, three fruit-bearers, and four small cottonwoods, flourished either side of a grape-arbor.

Enclosing this quiet ensemble, where the women trailed their skirts as they went about their homely tasks, a wire fence upheld the subtle rustle of honey-suckles and climbing roses.

The corral was nearly open field, with its light zinc roof to protect the vehicles, harness and fodder, its little yard with stalls for the horses, its chicken-coop which used up the trough-waste, and its adopted cur, not so harmless, despite the whimperings and snugglings of the little fellow.

Her name was Rosaura Torres and she was pretty. Her slippers slapped at her heels indolently like oriental sandals; her hands were skilled, her laughter eager, her dreams simple; life waited curious within her inviolate lips.

For her, every waking was gay, to live a daily boon, all flowers beautiful, the afternoons smiling and tranquil with something that cradled and soothed.

Rosaura was pretty and waiting to plunge her skilled hands into life, as into her morning basket of flowers.

IV

She had two blocks to go along the narrow sidewalk a meter above the dusty road, to reach the main street.

Rosaura walked out about five-thirty in her yellow dress, generously powdered, enjoying to the full all the usual incidents of her pilgrimage to the station, where she waited like the others for the six-thirty-five express.

At five-thirty Rosaura would leave, unaware of the miracle of youth that went with her. She crossed the end of the street, careful not to make a misstep in her Louis XV heels, and not to smudge with sandy soil the mirror perfection of her shoes. Half a block down she exchanged a good afternoon with old Petrona, who always stood on the threshold of her white house, her arms pillowed on the soft mound of her stomach, shaken with deep laughter.

"Hello, Doña Petrona."

"God bless you, child . . . why, you're a regular doll . . . poor boys! . . ."

Rosaura never heard the end, always crude banter, and she hurried the swift patter of her bright little shoes, knowing that at the corner masculine eyes would manage better to convey those flattering, but repellent, thoughts.

She was on the main street. Fashionable Lobos promenaded between station and plaza, its greetings and laughter ruffling the earlier silence of the streets.

The minutes flicked by spent in chatter, salvaged by charming or important ends. Words cloaked the feelings of the men and women who brushed each other—the women with the air of jewels on display, the men like wary customers concealing their tastes.

Rosaura

The afternoon would be winding itself out in dark corners, when the promenade, aimless heretofore, turned toward the station. Planks creaked in the floor of the waiting-room, through which the platform was gradually invaded.

And it was always the same, from the Bois de Boulogne with its tide of coughing motors to the modest echo of village heels, there in this last corner of the world, where tiny hopes waver up in a piteously simple society.

The station is to Lobos what Hyde Park is to London, the Retiro to Madrid, the Sweet Waters of Asia to Constantinople. If a slight, unknown guilt exists, it does not fall there.

But the first train is in. It is six o'clock, highest pitch of excitement till six-thirty-five, when the really important one, dealer of emotions from Buenos Aires, is due.

People passed, people criticized, and a web of romanticism entangled the youth of the town.

The minutes scrambled down the restless clock.

Rosaura saw that fashionable young man many times. Her friends teased her because of the insistent glances that they perhaps wished for themselves, and the girl felt something agreeably clouding her reason, when Carlos looked at her smiling, watching for recognition.

An emotion, greater than the little breast in the yellow dress, welled in Rosaura.

Through the restless days that speed too, the hours come again and again, and among them the moment when the express is due. The initials of an idyll can be traced on the dusty haunch of the cars, and Rosaura wrote her name on the diner, in which travelled the fashionable youth of the glance.

Oh, evil influence of the indifferent locomotive to whose monster eye the horizon presents no ideal! Pitiless train that passed on, abandoning to the monotonous boredom of the village those fanciful dreams of the sentimental Rosaura who wrote her fate on its cars!

But the enamoured child was too much a part of today's amazement to sense the disharmony between stable people and the great forces that pass. And one afternoon, when Carlos got down, ostensibly for a walk, and passed beside her very near, she felt she would fall, strangely drawn as if by the slight breath in his wake.

V

Little garden with your arbour, your odorous jasmine, your white and cold laurel and sexual carnations, something stirs there to fill you so tenderly. In Rosaura the simple provincial of pastoral soul, blooms the miracle of a great love.

Rosaura lives closing her eyes to possess more completely her intense emotion. Her coquetry is wasted no longer: for him her arms drop in consent; for him her pupils suffer this concentrated feeling; for him her body yields unknown surrender, when she walks wrapped in disturbing day-dreams; and for him too, her breast fills to the size of an entire world.

How enormous is this unsuspected world! At times Rosaura thinks and fears: What will be of her life now? Is this love? Does that incredibly elegant and distinguished youth love her too? She thinks and fears and leaves unsolved those impossible elusive problems.

Rosaura closes her eyes to possess more completely her intense emotion.

The days are no longer monotonous nor the hours leaden in that tiny unsuspected garden, there in the pampa that sings its endless song of the unending spaces.

And the spring that is not illusion brings the lilacs to bloom, clinging twined in clustered embraces, falling splendid in violet sprays; and in the vines that drooped from the eaves like slim and sensual boas, timid gleams of white jasmine appear. The honeysuckle too breathes a hint of the tropics, vibrant as a ringing bell; and the potted carnations burst into pride.

The soul of Rosaura wells an odour of troubled love like the perfumed wave of the honeysuckles. Her cheeks are like jasmine, her eyes become pooled to a sheen of grape, and her blood ripens her mouth so that she strangely needs to bite her lips.

The soul of Rosaura slowly is inhaled by her body.

Rosaura

VI

Restlessly wandering about, Rosaura awaits the unrealized idyll of those glances. Will he come? Won't he come?

She pictures beforehand, in the square of light framed by the car window, that fine profile hastily looking up from the paper to seek her alone, among all the girls of the crowded platform.

Always it is his tense eyes that pierce her, fixed on her black locks, on her shoulders, on her walk which suddenly shifts with mysterious languor.

To look into his face is a physical shock and just to think of his face flushes her cheeks, and makes her mind grow dangerously wild. She fears then she may walk crookedly, may fall absurdly on account of a misstep, or because of that moment's blindness may run blankly into someone who would guess her disturbance.

Carrying these painfully intense visions, Rosaura walks arm in arm with her friends, and plunges into dreadfully flat talk to hide and disguise them.

But the green tranquil light becomes a red, color

of blood and passion. Two meters above the rails the monster eye of the locomotive runs flaming brighter, and then passes beyond, as the steely forehead of the engine turns to the horizon. There is the shock of yielding metal. Rosaura suffers, arm in arm with her friends indifferently lost in Sunday laughter.

And one afternoon—strange!—when she sought in the frame of the window that profile which had been to her an intangible, fugitive ideal calling forth dreams, and no more, she saw the man descend with his great suitcase; stride across the crowd on the platform, and take a cab of old Torres, with the gesture of a landlord returning to his estate.

Rosaura felt her soul pierced by the anguish of a virgin possessed.

She was displeased by the active, direct, now justified teasing of her friends. She left them with scant caresses to flutter the streets with their stale and flat chatter, and fled home in amaze, fearful and dazzled as a quail.

Rosaura

VII

Rosaura slept badly all that night, pursued by a vague event whose influence would definitely change her life.

Already roused she heard her father in the kitchen, splitting wood for the morning *mate*.

She joined the old man, surprising him with that unnecessary rising.

"Where will the sun come up?"

"It's you, daddy, that woke me."

"Well, go on out to the hen-coop and bring in some kindling."

Dawn lighted the yard when Rosaura in quest of the chips saw Lucio's coach ready to leave.

"I'm going to the hotel, *niña*, to get a stranger who's come to look at *haciendas*."

"And why the extra harness?"

"Seems we're goin' to go far . . . maybe till tonight."

Lucio twisted his half-open mouth and clapped his tongue on his palate, clucking the horses to start: the uneven team disappeared through the gate, the coach seemed to drop in a hole, comical and shameless as a street wench.

"Good-bye, *niña!*"

The coachman had exaggerated; when Rosaura went down toward the main street that afternoon, after speaking to Doña Petrona, she was struck with surprise upon seeing Carlos seated at a small table in front of the hotel, accompanied by the political leader Barrios, the cattle-auctioneer Gonzalez, the representative Iturri and other gentlemen of the hour.

Naturally Carlos bowed to her like the rest and Rosaura answered courteously though she felt naked in her blushes. How hard to maintain a natural walk and how awful to linger like that before ten staring men!

Rosaura's pride suffered and the susceptible little creole, hurt by that supposedly betraying blush, hated the stranger violently. Why couldn't things remain as they were, easy?

She was overcome by a fear of having to talk to Carlos in public. She believed her platform flirtation so flagrant. . . .

Rosaura

Oh, indeed! she would make him pay for that humiliation doubtless already glossed by the clumsy words of that shameless crowd in front of the Hotel de Paris; nobody should have a peg on which to hang a tale about *her* favours.

And that afternoon at the glory hour of Lobos, Rosaura, wounded in the privacy of her romantic passion, became singularly talkative and attentive to the chatter of her friends, returned their shafts charmingly, and cruelly, suicidally ridiculed the elegant youth, who followed her with his eyes fixed steadily as the headlights of an automobile on the road.

When Rosaura went home she was exhausted and convinced that she had been uselessly a coward; she threw herself on the bed and, pathetically dishevelled, wept great sobs of pain for her blighted passion.

VIII

Fortunately that state of affairs did not last. Rosaura would have died of grief. It was not possible to weep so, days and days, accusing herself bitterly.

199

Tales from the Argentine

Carlos had left on the morning following that, to him, incomprehensible afternoon.

No actions proved, and no words even, that the saucy flirtation of the girl on the platform meant anything more than a few moments' diversion. Hurt by the impudence of the staring little chit in the yellow dress, he thought no more of the matter, unaware that he left a great passion tortured into a sorrow, as the train jerked from the station in the biting chill of that windy morning.

In the garden that smelled of jasmine, honeysuckle and carnations, little Rosaura wilted like a flower bruised by some casual humming-bird which flitted on, once it had sucked the savor.

Ended for ever, the gay starts every afternoon at five; the hellos to Doña Petrona; the coquettishly careful crossings; the fastidious resentment at the brutal stares of the loungers in front of the Hotel de Paris, the meetings with her friends and the glorified walks on the platform, before those eyes that kindled her and pierced her.

There was nothing left but to weep, weep for-ever, for these memories of her broken life.

Rosaura

Rosaura would have died had she thought that the fashionable youth of the dining car would never come back, or would pass in the train as indifferent to her as the monster eye of the locomotive to the ideal of the horizon.

It was five. Rosaura recalled even the slightest movements of her habit of years and years. Impatience pulled her to the dressing-table, but a presentiment of martyrdom dropped her on her knees before the niche adorned with palms crossed ovally, where her little blue madonna spangled with gold prayed, in mystic stance, through the centuries.

Oh, that he might be returned to her with a smile of forgiveness; that she might receive only two affectionate lines so as not to die strangled by this thing so much bigger than herself!

Three dry little knocks of somebody's knuckles on the door announced a discreet visitor. Rosaura hurriedly arranged her pitifully disordered self, and in came Carmen, the friend of the pink dress who had been deserted so long, in the distress of that wrecked love. And as Rosaura's arms passionately convulsive about her were a confession, Carmen, charmingly comforting, spoke openly:

"Holy Mother, be still! . . . why, I've a piece of news that will just make you laugh!"

Rosaura, turned to the wall to hide her tears, quivered from head to foot and her shoulders shook with deep, painful sobs.

"Don't cry like that. . . . You'd do better to start making a peach of a dress for the dance that the Club is giving next week. . . . Or don't you care?"

"Don't joke with me, Carmen."

"Joke? Sit down and listen to real information. . . . I know who he is, what he thinks of you, what he came for and a lot of other things."

"And who told you all that?"

"Gonzalez, who showed him the cows for Lorenzo Ramallo."

"And what's he got to do with Ramallo?"

"Nothing much, he's his son, that's all."

Far from being overcome by that name known far and wide as one of the cream of landholders, Rosaura's passion rose with this new impossibility.

Rosaura

So long as Carlos passed through on the train, so long as he came now and then to the isolated little village of Lobos, so long as he looked at her as he had, her love would seek more impulses to grow.

"What else did he say?" she murmured tremblingly.

"That you're a marvel and that he's coming to the dance at the Club to meet you. Now cry if you want!"

Rosaura did not weep but she paled unbelievably. She suffered a torment of pleasure and that fulfillment was as painful as a pregnancy.

More than ever the rings deepened under her eyes, beneath her drooped eyelids; and while Carmen ran merrily on, a smile rose to her lips from the calm depths of her love in contemplation.

IX

Came a tranquil time to the Torres place. The little garden sprouted under the caress of the sun. The orchard bore amply either side of the arboured vine. The red-crested ceibo tree scattered fine

205

glints in the shimmering air. The dog chased mischievously around the edges of feminine skirts, balancing the silver notes of its little whimper like a tune rehearsed in a nightingale's nest.

On the porch enclosed by the fresh bloom of its vines, Rosaura sewed leaning back in her chair. Patches of sunlight dropped on the dress through the vines and the leaves overhead; and when with an indolent foot she would start the chair rocking, those imperceptible wavelets of warmth ran carelessly over her body.

At her right a bent-legged sewing-basket spread out like a split nut, its contents brimming, and on the left a little table unevenly set on the flags, threatened to drop a fashion review lent by a friend on one of the estates for the occasion of the Club dance.

Happy, the lovely Rosaura, absorbed in her work, threaded promises of her love on the porch shaded by the quiet garden stirred in the spring.

Rosaura had chosen from among the models a pattern of muslin embroidered with buds and sprays of fern fine as cobwebs. It opened a bare timid triangle at the neck and a great sash with a bow on one side fluffed like a full rose.

How much she knew now of the Carlos heretofore so mysterious and so untold! Carlos had been educated in Europe. On his return Don Lorenzo, his father, had given him the place at General Alvear to manage, which however did not hinder later travels into countries fabulous to Rosaura.

What a new wreath of glory all of this laid upon him, in the heart of the romantic little provincial!

She would go with him as in the fairy-tales, to enchanting and beautiful lands where everything is as easy as dreaming and where to love is to fulfill the most sacred duty. Her hand would be held in his and he would tell her about everything, knowing everything. Then they would return to the little garden, and would live in the neighborhood that reminded them of other days.

Rosaura ran the needle into her finger. One of the buds on the muslin blushed deeper, and she, annoyed at this stupid break in her rhythmic trance, pressed the tip of the hurt finger, making a tiny crimson source.

The dress was finished on time.

x

The greyish façade of the Club Social occupied twenty yards of the cobble-stoned street; from its windows streamed a blaze of festive light, promising gaiety.

At nine that night the hearts of the Lobos girls beat fast, this being the hour to put the last touches on the frocks that would mean scorn or envy. Only Rosaura, pale as a bride, shivers running over her body in its spring-time festoon of sprays and buds, remained indifferent to such petty social successes.

She had arrayed herself with the delicate care of a miniaturist, drawing on the long stiff silk hose, finished off by the bright patent-leather pumps; her skin had quivered at the touch of the fine white undergarment spangled with yellow bows, fitted snugly to her torso by the girdle, rose-faint as a blush. And she had called her mother to gaze as she slipped into the rustling folds of the frock.

Rosaura

It was time. She walked toward the mirror tasting, at the measured swing of her step, the barely tangible subtlety of her airy garments; she walked profiled, light as an apparition; smiled faintly, lifting in quick amazement her mobile eyebrows; and she thought she might please because of that shade of docility in her eyes, messengers of miracles.

It was time and she was ready, pure and vibrant as a crystal shivered by the distant note of a bronze bell. She swooned almost, with virginal ripeness of sacrifice, sensing herself worshipped by the intact garments, adorned with the solemn splendours of an offering. "Oh, yes, all his." And a momentary loss of consciousness sent her swaying for support to the bureau, where her hand, limp and cold, lay like marble on the red glamour of the mahogany.

"Come on, come on! . . ." The door opened filling the room with brief clamour. The Gomez girls had arrived to fetch her, as agreed, and Rosaura folded in on herself, like a sensitive plant.

In the dance-hall of the Club Social, revealed

inconsiderately by the hard, blinding lights, the reception committee, self-conscious and solemn, fenced opportunely.

Carlos, acquainted with the gloved punctiliousness of such parties, had come early, to settle himself comfortably in a private corner.

An air of naïve cordiality already reigned, and they had all become more used to the gala dress, when the auctioneer Gonzalez, waving a hand from left to right, spoke their names softly:

"Señor Carlos Ramallo, Señorita Rosaura Torres."

To Rosaura, that coupling of their names attained the significance of a question before the altar.

"Very pleased, señor," she said, and she thought this was everything.

He gave her his arm properly.

"As to me I confess it was almost absolutely necessary to speak to you, since I look upon you as an old friend."

Rosaura blushed:

"It is true, we have seen each other so often."

Rosaura

Oh, the melodious enchantment of walking thus, arm in arm, with their words moving close to confession!

And all Lobos looking on!

"Shall we sit down?"

"If you like."

They went out through the corridor, toward a bench glimpsed in the patio, suddenly glorified by the luminous glitter of stars, in a sky framed by the naïve grey cornice.

"This is nice."

They sat down, relieved of pretense; night knows nothing of etiquette and love is everywhere, naturally.

They were silent. Rosaura, quiet, looking at the button of her glove and in the comradely tone that the night required, queried:

"Tell me about yourself. Would you mind? I have lived so alone here."

Carlos did not reply. To tell the child, simple as a red bloom, of his intricate fashionable adventures would be the irreverent action of a cheap Don Juan.

"Please believe my amusements don't amount to anything."

"But—and all you have travelled in this wide world?"

"I have some pleasant memories."

And carried away in the mood of Rosaura, who intently waited for wondrous tales, he seemed to have just discovered the true charm of things past.

He was surprised to hear himself saying sincerely:

"Those journeys are saddening when one makes them alone."

With what further absurdities would he continue?

But Rosaura, surmising an indirect allusion, toyed more intently with her glove, purchased for the ball.

Scenting a new fad, other couples followed Carlos and Rosaura toward the patio, and the night, its silence broken, was dethroned. Carlos recalled other scenes trilled too with laughter and dizzied with perfumes.

"Will you dance?"

Rosaura

But another youth claimed that polka from Rosaura. Carlos found himself alone and near his friend the auctioneer, so he begged to be presented to other girls, saying to himself that thus he would mask his reason for coming to the dance.

The daughter of Barrios was a lovely wench of excited voice, from whose pouter-pigeon bosom gushed a tangle of the most astonishing speeches.

What a relief, what a pleasure, when he found himself again with the simple Rosaura, love entire, on a bench in the patio now emptied by the greed that free refreshments awakened!

"Oh, señorita, how your friends weary me!"

"Don't call me señorita."

"Thank you, Rosaura, how all these little Sunday girls bore me. If I couldn't feel myself a friend of yours, I would dash out at a gallop. Stay with me awhile, as long or as short as you please, and I shall be grateful."

"You see how quickly we understand each other," laughed Rosaura. "But unfortunately I would have to hear tales if I stayed as long as I'd like."

"Would it be very long?"

Rosaura turned again to the button of her glove, and they were silent, overcome by discoveries mutually guessed.

One must, when one cannot speak from the soul, touch on simple things to hear undisturbed the song within.

"Are you always bored, Rosaura?"

"Not before. I had enough with my work and my walks to the station or to the plaza, where I met my friends and we would amuse ourselves with our jokes and our foolishness. Now I want more. The town seems so dreary, and I think of how you travel so much, have seen so many things. . . ."

"And yet you see I come here."

To say something, terrified by the consequences of her own words, Rosaura murmured:

"You must have a reason."

"Don't you know it?"

"Why should I know it?"

Rosaura was suffering now. Carlos' eyebrows were drawn tightly together, hardening his expression. Something vaguely in his smile prophesied who knows what dreadful phrase.

Rosaura

"Please, Carlos, be still."

The eyebrows were calmed, the forced smile disappeared:

"We do not need to say much."

It was true, and as the fraternally begun conversation had turned difficult, Carlos again told stories of his restless life to the little provincial so childishly attuned with her trustful eyes.

This intimate chat bridged a long time easily, and then Carlos with the air of a guardian said:

"Well, go and dance now with your friends, or they'll be saying that we are sweethearts."

"Oh, heavens!"

"Anyhow we are good friends."

"Yes, . . . but now, who knows when you'll come back."

"You'll see. . . . I have it arranged so that it won't be so seldom."

Rosaura went back to the hall, leaving Carlos without thinking to ask him to explain.

And thus ended the first meeting of the provincial girl with the elegant youth of the diner, now a cordial friend: which is not little for an ideal that passes, rousing great dreams that can never come true.

XI

From then on, after that night so brimful of lover's portent, the six-thirty-five express no longer carried an intangible ideal, the youth of the diner in his frame of light. Carlos had found a better solution and sacrificing the sluggishness of a bad sleeper, took the train at five in the morning to spend the day in Lobos.

The pretexts, though weak, would suffice: To see his friend the auctioneer Gonzalez, to go uselessly to his sales, or simply to shorten the six monotonous hours of the usual journey.

But what are pretexts when two lives are drawn to each other?

The sun was high when Carlos descended hampered by his London suitcase checkered with hotel labels.

Scarcely anybody stood on the platform, so crowded in the half-hour between the two express-trains, the six o'clock and the six-thirty-five. One of old Torres' cabs took him to the Hotel de Paris

where he "made the morning" with **Gonzalez,**
Iturri, and other personages of the hour. He
lunched with the appetite of a traveller and slept a
restful siesta till four, when he took tea facing the
cobble-stoned street which fluttered already in pros-
pect of the daily promenade.

And all this just for the little half hour in the
afternoon, in the teeming confusion of the crowded
platform: politicians out on campaign, young men
in gray felts and light shoes, personages displaying
their official personalities, sheiks with straw hats
about to slide off their greasy foreheads and stickily
pomaded skulls, coachmen waiting for fares, peons
for mail or on errands. While like aromatic blooms
in a virgin forest, the Lobos girls passed flirtatious
and mocking.

From end to end of the platform, flanked by
her friends, the one in pink and the one in sky-
blue, Rosaura walked with the tread of a co-
quette, returning the glances of Carlos, her
affectionate friend, with smiles that opened like
flowers.

And Carlos filled his eyes with that dainty loved

figure which retreated as if in anger, or gazed into those docile pupils open and penetrable as windows wide to a tryst.

But the cars of the express clanked unevenly in. The asthmatic gasps of the locomotive died down.

The blazing train drew up in front of the covered station and shut out the night.

People ascended, people descended, the minutes scrambled down the restless clock; on the dusty haunch of the diner, while speaking her last shy words of farewell, Rosaura traced the initials of an idyll. And suddenly, tearing a great wound through the soul of the little enamoured provincial, a brutal screech announced the departure. The cars flew apart like the vertebræ of a reptile in flight; the iron of joints and bumpers clanged from locomotive to caboose. Carlos bowed, quickly smaller at a sudden distance. The caboose passed rapidly, striking from the station windows a vibrant near echo.

And before Rosaura rose the deep indifference of the spangled night, painfully stifling the fugitive blare of the train which flies with the blind gaze of its monster eye toward the horizon whose attraction it does not comprehend.

Poor little Rosaura, abandoned thus to that passion too large for herself, in the deadly boredom of the village lost in a pampa that ignores the way of romance in its children.

XII

Nevertheless, except for the disconsolate parting that wounded as if it were forever, Rosaura's life overflowed happiness.

In her garden now heightened beyond spring-time budding, the lilac dropped great fragrant sprays and the fresh porch flourished green, spattered with morning-glories, jasmines and honey-suckle.

Yielding to the soft breath of summer, Rosaura dreamed warmly through the stream of hours.

Seated in her rocking-chair, bathed in the odour of flowers, she works without ceasing, the needle quick in her skilled hands.

At her right, the sewing-basket on its bent legs spreads open like a split nut, its contents brimming.

To her left, a little table unevenly set on the flags holds scattered colourful fashion books borrowed from that friend who had sent her the first for the dance at the Club Social.

Happy beyond explanation, the little Rosaura intent on her work lives with memories of meetings with her beloved Carlos so worthy of all the passions.

Rosaura had many patterns because she had quickly found herself deplorably provincial in her country clothing. And what feminine delight to devote all her days thus to sheathing herself in chaste caressing undergarments. Oh, the bows and the weaves white as holy wafers around her virgin body, all an offering to the mysterious rites of adoration! Gentle murmurs of future bliss steal into her dreams. She would be worthy of him, simple and naïve but still passionate and tender in the radiant fire of a love all immolation.

Elusively identical the days passed in the little garden of the Torres stables, idealized by the intense soul of Rosaura, always certain that her Carlos would come tomorrow, day after tomorrow, or next

week, to tell her with his eyes that he loved her, put
in her hand a nosegay of strange country blossoms,
and in the afternoon to take a departure as painful
as if forever, but to return because that was fate.

XIII

Night knowing something of sorcery transformed
the insipid plaza of the town. Night, the blue, the
stars; reducing the visible world to a few pools of
light wept by the lamps, immobile, isolate and sad,
condemned to stay forever, although they aspire
desperately to be stars: a desire aroused by the
springtime infinity of the depthless sky.

The people, limited to their bodies, tread the
slavery of the plaza paths made to walk on, and
cannot escape in perishable desires.

And so their souls fling themselves into mad impossible futures and migrate from love to love, as
does light from star to star, drilling through the.
spaces that bar the victory of matter.

But it is the same plaza. The bushes and hedges
clipped like thick manes shape greenish-black geo-
metric figures curiously similar to human forms.

The paths curve, lacking space in which to be true
roads that know where they are going. A few trees,
newly green, have become thus tender in response to
the benison of spring, on time as always.

The groups of girls are like displays under
glass of souls that will love, and the men long im-
possibly to clasp a bunch of them with feverish
hands.

Carlos comes when he can to this holiday parade
on the plaza stretched out under the stars, beneath
the holy watch of the colonial bell-tower, where
with infinite forgiveness God blesses his straying
sentimental lambs.

In that luminous scene of fans, skirts and blouses,
the most beautiful is Rosaura and also the farthest
from herself; for she is carried off by great dreams
of a heroine of romance, pining for the hero who
has appeared from an unbelievable land, with a halo
of the glamorous unknown.

Oh! . . . To be thus chosen among all!

Night, that knows something of sorcery, filters its
temptation into the hearts of those people, who, God
be thanked, have their morals; that is why this tale

does not end here, with the most natural of love's solutions.

XIV

Thus Rosaura reached the height of her glory. Carlos' intervals of absence were brief, in which to savour every word, every gesture; and their meetings were fulfillments whose intuitive comprehensions made vows superfluous; rapture floated around them, as if exhaled by their emotions.

But that state of their souls perhaps called disaster upon them, as lightning is drawn by the crosses that pray on cupolas.

Carlos, pretending to take the matter lightly, told her he was leaving shortly for Europe:

". . . Oh! For a very short time; three or four months at the most . . . through the summer . . . I can't avoid it; my father would be very much surprised and he might even be angry . . ."

Rosaura, mortally wounded, listened with anguish.

"Tell me, Carlos. Isn't Señor Ramallo sending you away?"

"What an idea, child! And why should he?"

"Don't know . . . maybe they've told him that you're wasting your time in some little village."

"No, Rosaura, what a notion!"

Carlos explained again. Who would know and if they did, who would think anything bad of his visits to Lobos? But it meant much to his father for him to make this trip to England, where he would learn a great deal studying the best-known model farms under a competent person.

"Three or four months . . . it seems so long, Carlos!"

He answered her, for the first time with a plain meaning:

"Rosaura, believe me, even if I were gone six, they would be too few to erase certain things."

"Sure?"

"Very sure."

Life sprang again in the little village girl. Carlos spoke with so much assurance that his absence seemed more bearable, and the especially tender pitch of that beloved voice was deceptive balm to her sensitive soul. Furthermore, Rosaura possessed the greatness of noble trust, and an extraordinary feminine delight in sacrificing herself to the will of her idol. In her eyes Carlos could do nothing wrong. And that poor night they parted; their hands more than ever revealed their love, despite all human obstacles.

XV

It was summer, and of Carlos nothing remained in Lobos except the increasing passion of his Rosaura and a brief note of farewell in her hands.

Life went on as usual in the Torres household, except for the lengthened burdensome days, the greater fatigue of the horses and the always perspiring peons, the sleepy inertia of the throbbing siesta hour, and the sadness of the poor girl, drooping now like a flower prostrated by the full blaze of the sun.

Nevertheless, her faith firm in her Carlos, Rosaura laboured to embellish herself. Her provincial wardrobe disappeared totally and no one, by her clothing, could have distinguished the former showy little country girl in yellow from a fashionable urban young lady.

This clothing that wove its knowing charms

around her was born of the wish to seem elegant to him, and its contact filled, though imperfectly, the void left by the want of other caresses.

How daring dreams are; and how, by sheer familiarity with her more and more definite visions of what might happen, Rosaura grew to feel that she had been incredibly timid.

She did not know how, but she was certain that on Carlos' return their love would take a more natural course, and this prodded her anxious count of the long days.

But time passed with all its apparent slowness, while Rosaura worked to make herself beautiful, cared for her person as for an idol that belonged to someone else, and for whose pricelessness she was responsible. At this stage she never doubted the love of her Carlos.

XVI

An incurable sadness floated in the little garden of the Torres place, breathed off by the approaching winter that blighted the flowers so merrily brought by the spring.

Rosaura

The autumn petals were seared by the cold, the last stunted peaches dropped from their boughs, the arbour was stripped of its grapes and the little garden so piteously rifled bore a seal of arid harshness.

A mild patch of sunlight filtered on the porch, overhung by once matted vines, gilding the withered leaves. Rosaura, pale with her first woman's sorrow, had lost her youthful jasmine smoothness and her honeysuckle lushness; and abetted by sleepless outpourings of tears, the violet rings under her eyes triumphantly deepened to the transparent sheen of grapes.

Poor little Rosaura, tender aimless fancy; the fragrance of whose love was worthy of immortalizing a whole town's prosaic staleness.

Poor little Rosaura, victim of a moment of fateful evolution; incurable longing of simple things for the meshes of splendor; on her simple faith in the promise of a beyond, turned all her disaster.

Her fate was to suffer and no other, because thus says a homely proverb: "Who looks too far upward may break his neck."

Her grief was as fatal as the race of melting snow downward.

Immensely sad is the little garden of the Torres place. From the soul of its small mistress disconsolate dreams ebb, while autumn falls like a shroud upon that corner of the world, lost in the middle of the changeless pampa that knows nothing of romantic loves.

XVII

A nervous anxiety aroused Rosaura from the dejection in which she lived. Carlos might come any moment.

The daughter of Crescencio Torres returned to her old habits and except for Carmen or whoever in the village possessed the gift of divination, Lobos ignored the change in the spirit of its lovely child.

About five-thirty Rosaura went out in an airy blouse, cut triangularly at the neck, dark blue skirt, and calf pumps, though bareheaded so as not to be too conspicuous among her friends. Half a block down she stopped to speak to old Petrona unweariedly standing on the threshold of her white house, her arms pillowed on the soft mound of her stomach shaken with deep laughter.

"Hello, Doña Petrona."

"God bless you, child. . . . My, the poor boys, you're a regular poster! . . . Holy Mary! why you're right up to the minute! . . ."

But Rosaura would not hear.

On the main street, fashionable Lobos promenaded, fluttering with chatter the paths shaded by hoary elms.

Afternoon would be winding itself out in the corners when they gradually invaded the crowded platform.

What an unbearable emotion, this waiting; what torment and overcoming reminder arose in Rosaura at the gleam of the headlight of the locomotive on the rails!

Yes, he will come this afternoon. She will spy him in his window, meeting her with brilliant joy in his eyes. Her soul will divine his presence and all her old delight will burst forth like a radiant dawn.

"Oh, to fall in his arms!"

But in the glaring frame of that window which once gave life, no face appeared.

XVIII

The leaves fell, the first chill crept out, and Rosaura suffered like the red autumn blooms that freeze in the flight of the sun.

Was all that romance an illusion?

The poor girl almost believed so, with the daily disappointment of the vacant space in the window of the diner.

But it was not an illusion, because one afternoon when her heart was breaking, Carmen took her by the arm and trembling at the enormity of her announcement said:

"Come here, child, come, I've seen him in another car."

Oh, Rosaura! How to keep a scream from escaping? Her legs refused to advance, though her friend dragged her by the arm. It was true, he was there.

Carlos! . . . Oh, to fall on his beloved breast and to tell him that she never doubted his return, and then so many, many things more! She recognized him through a dim window. Nearly swooning, and almost stretching out her arms, there before them all, her upper-lip rose smiling faintly; and he bowed merely, as if there had never existed between them anything beyond a passing word.

XIX

Rosaura fell into a coma of intense pain. Everybody in the house knew that something unusual had happened to her and the mother learned of the drama on the delirious night that followed the incident unperceived by others.

The love of Rosaura, rooted in her like an organism inseparable from her own, was killing her with its death.

Carmen, the friend who had once brought the first-fruits of her love, brought her the gravestone as well:

"Listen, child . . . it isn't worth while, suffering for that wicked man."

"Please, Carmen, let's not speak of it any more."

"It's that I wanted to tell you . . . if you want to notice next time he passes, you'll see that he is with another woman, all dressed up in those things that you like."

"For God's sake be still, Carmen."

So she swallowed the details which her friend brought to be close to her; livid, her lips quivering childishly but with her eyes dry, she burst into sobs long and painful as if her very bowels were being dragged from her slowly.

XX

Rosaura has come to the station, in her frock of flowered muslin, reminder of that unforgettable night in the Club Social. She has tucked the brief note, the only one from Carlos, in her bosom, the note of farewell, and her convulsive hands crumble to dust the dry petals of the flowers she had kept because he had given them to her.

Rosaura must be a little mad to come dressed like that to the platform. But what does she care what they say?

Carmen is with her, caring for her like a nurse,

232

troubled by those strange fancies, and dressed as always in pink, not having suffered, like her friend, the intense influence of outside things.

Suddenly, Rosaura's hand sinks into the soft flesh of her friend's arm.

"Come on, Carmen, come on for God's sake, I can't stand any more."

Thus together they walked to the end of the platform. Carlos (oh, horrible unconsciousness!) rides in a compartment with the unknown woman and Rosaura does not want to see him.

"Oh, I can't bear any more, I can't bear any more . . . and leave me now, I beg you for the sake of what you love most . . . leave me and go back with the rest, I'm going home."

"But, child, you don't want me to leave you, and you in that state and crying like a lost soul?"

"Yes, for the sake of what you love most, leave me."

What powerful influence made Carmen obey?

The shrill locomotive announces departure. Carmen goes back to the station.

There is a shock of steel, the locomotive snorts its

great poisonous crests out upon Lobos, gasping a strenuous start. The train will continue its journey from unknown to unknown, from horizon to horizon.

Then the little Rosaura, overcome by a terrible madness, screams, grinding incomprehensible

phrases between her teeth that clamp convulsively with pain. And like a springtime butterfly she flashes out, running between the parallel infinities of the rails, her arms forward in useless offering, calling the name of Carlos, for whom it is passionate joy to die, on the road that takes him away, far from her forever.

"Carlos! . . . Carlos! . . ."

The steely din nears her. The swift victory of

Rosaura

the train knows nothing of the cries of a passion
that knew how to die.

"Carlos! . . ."

And like a snowy feather, the dainty figure in
flowered muslin yields to the march of the gigantic
locomotive, for whose monster eye the horizon holds
no ideal.

7. THE RETURN OF ANACONDA

Horacio Quiroga

Horacio Quiroga, like Lugones, lives today in Buenos Aires: he is as pre-eminent in the art of the short story as Lugones in the poem: and like Lugones again he is removed from the current literary movements of the day—movements in which Güiraldes was a leader. The locale of the best of Quiroga's tales is the Chaco, a wedge of dense subtropical land between Paraguay and Brazil. He is a master in the depiction of the dwellers, human and animal, in these luxuriant wastes. Quiroga's animal tales, of course, have been likened to those of Kipling—a comparison as inevitable as it is superficial. Kipling's method, in his jungle tales, is "realism"—a sophisticated pastiche of the animals "as they are." The South American's method is at once more naïve and more profound. He makes no attempt at an impossible verisimilitude. He depicts his animals, as the Italian primitives depicted Biblical scenes, with the intent not of accuracy but of an æsthetic portrayal of a human universal truth. Such tales as this that follows articulate the movement of the jungle-life with a directness that is closer to music than to the conventional story.

This tale is taken from "Los Desterrados" (The Exiles).

The Return of Anaconda

WHEN Anaconda, in conjunction with the native elements of the jungle, planned the reconquest of the river, she had just reached her thirtieth year.

She was a young serpent ten meters long and in her prime. Throughout her vast hunting grounds there was no deer or jaguar whose breath could withstand her embrace. Wrung to death, all life dissolved in her braced muscles. The swaying grass that marked the trail of the great boa stiffened the entire jungle, raised and pointed its ears. And when at twilight in the quiet hours Anaconda bathed her ten meters of dark velvet in the fiery river, silence encircled her like a halo.

But Anaconda's presence did not always displace life before it, like a deadly gas. Her peaceful movements, unsensed by men, were hailed at a distance by the animals. Like this:

"Good day," Anaconda would say to the alligators, as she passed through the swamps.

"Good day," the beasts would answer mildly in the sun, laboriously forcing the sealed clay from their eyelids.

"It is going to be warm today," the perched monkeys would greet her, aware from the bowed underbrush of the great serpent's glide.

"Yes, very warm," Anaconda would answer, and draw after her the gaze and chatter of the monkeys, only half assured.

Because monkey and serpent, bird and snake, rat and reptile, are fatal pairs which even the terror of great hurricanes and the drain of interminable droughts can hardly pacify. Only a mutual adjustment to common conditions which has been wrought and bequeathed from immemorial days can ever override in times of catastrophe that deadly pattern of hunger. And so, in a great drought, the anguished flamingo, the turtles, the rats and the anacondas will chorus one lament for a drop of water.

When we found our Anaconda, the wretched jungle was about to create once more this somber brotherhood.

For two months back no rain had crackled on the dusty leaves. Even the dew, life and comfort of the scorched bush, had disappeared. Night after night, from sundown to sundown, the land baked as if it were a giant oven. The beds of fresh streams had become a stubble of smooth, burning stones; and the thick sloughs of dark water and rotting trunks were now raised clay beds furrowed with hardened tracks webbed across like weaver's waste; and this was all that was left of the great floating jungle. Along the edge of the woods cacti, upright as candelabra, drooped now with their arms hanging to the hard dry earth that echoed the slightest shock.

One after one the days slid hazily by in a fog of distant fires, under the flame of a sky white to blindness, across which a yellow rayless sun moved toward the afternoon, when it began to drop wrapped in vapour like an enormous snuffed live coal.

Anaconda's vagabond life need not have been much affected by the drought. Beyond the lake and her shrunken pools, toward the rising sun, flowed her great native river, the refreshing Paranahyba, which she could have reached in any half-day.

But the boa no longer went to her river. Once, as far as the memory of her ancestors stretched, the river had been hers. Water, bush, wolves, storms and solitude, she had possessed it all.

Not now. One man first, with his beggarly lust of seeing, touching, stripping, had appeared around the sand bar in his long pirogue. Then other men, and still more, each time at shorter intervals. And all of them filthy smelling, filthy with *machetes* and ceaseless fires. And always following the river, to the south. . . .

Many days from there, the Paranahyba was given another name, she well knew. But beyond that, toward the unknowable gulf of water forever descending, would there not be an end, an immense shoal across, to stop the waters eternally falling?

From there, surely, must come the men, and the wedges, and the wandering mules that infected the jungle. If she could close the Paranahyba, restore its savage silence, and again delight as before, when she crossed the river whistling on dark nights, her head three meters above the foaming waters! . . .

Yes; raise a barrier to wall the river.

And suddenly she thought of the logs.

Anaconda's years were short; but she knew of two or three floods that had poured into the Paraná millions of uptorn trees and aquatic plants bubbling with mire. Where had it all settled and rotted? What tomb could contain the fleet of logs which a flood like none before might burst over the rim of that unknown gulf?

She recalled perfectly; rise of 1883; flood of 1894. . . . And given the eleven years since without great rains, the tropic like herself in her very jaws must feel thirst for a deluge.

Her ophidian sensitiveness to the atmosphere rippled hope through her scales. She felt the deluge near. And like another Peter the Hermit, Anaconda launched her crusade, all along the little rivers and fluvial streams.

The drought in her haunts was not, it is understood, uniform throughout the vast basin. So that at the end of long journeys, her nostrils expanded at the heavy moisture of the swamps, levels of water-bloom, and at the faint formic breath of the tiny ants that tunnelled intricately through them.

It was not hard for Anaconda to persuade the animals. Man has been, is and will be the cruelest enemy of the jungle.

"Then if we can close the river," concluded Anaconda, having detailed her plan at length, "men can no longer reach us."

"But the rains we need?" the water-rats objected, unable to hide their doubts. "We don't know whether they will fall!"

"They'll come! And before you imagine it! I know!"

"She knows it," the snakes affirmed. "She has lived among men. She knows them."

"Yes, I know them. And I know that a single

log, only one, if it runs in a great rise, drags with it the grave of one man."

"I should say so!" the snakes suavely smiled. "And maybe of two . . ."

"Or five," an old jaguar yawned from his flanks. "But tell me," he stretched directly toward Anaconda, "are you sure there will be enough logs to dam the river? I ask just to be asking . . ."

"Well, of course, these, nor all that can rise for two hundred leagues around, will not be enough. . . . But I confess you have put the only question that troubles me. No, brothers! All the logs of the basin of the Paranahyba and the Rio Grande do Sul with all their tributaries, will not be enough to jam a ten-league bar across the river. If I could not count on more, I would long since have stretched myself across the path of the first scout with a *machete*. . . . But I have great hopes of the rains falling everywhere and flooding the valley of the Paraguay. You don't know it . . . it is a grand river. If it rains there, as inevitably it will rain here, our victory is certain. Brothers: there are piles of logs up there in those waters we could never traverse, not in the whole sum of our lives!"

"Quite," the alligators agreed in a heavy drowse. "That is a lovely country. . . . But how will we know if it does rain there? We have weak little feet . . ."

"No, poor things . . ." Anaconda smiled, exchanging an ironic glance with the water-hogs squatted ten prudent meters off. "We shan't make you go so far. . . . I think just any fowl can reach us from there, in three flights, to bring us the good news. . . ."

"We aren't just any fowls," said the toucans, "and we shall come in a hundred flights, because we fly very badly. And we are not afraid of anybody. And we shall come flying, because nobody makes us, and we want to. And we aren't afraid of anybody." Breathless, the toucans stared at the others stolidly, with their great golden eyes framed in blue.

"It is we who are afraid," a grey eaglet squealed to the piper, sleepily fluffing itself.

"Not of you, nor of anybody. We fly in short

laps; but afraid, no . . ." the toucans insisted, calling the others again to witness.

"Yes, yes," Anaconda put in, for the dispute grew bitter, as always bitter have been the jungle discussions of abilities. "Nobody is afraid of anybody, and we all know it. . . . And the admirable toucans will come then, and tell us when it has rained in the other basin."

"We'll do it because we please; but nobody makes us," repeated the toucans.

"If this goes on," thought Anaconda, "the whole plan will soon be forgotten."

"Brothers!" with a stinging whistle she reared herself, "we are wasting our time. We are all equals, but together. Each one of us, by himself, is not much. United, we are the jungle. Brothers, let us hurl the jungle upon man! He destroys everything. He leaves nothing unstripped and unfilthied! The river will bear all our tropics, with its rains, its animals, its logs, its fevers and its snakes! Let us hurl the bush through the river, till we choke it! We shall tear ourselves away, die, if we need to, but let us hurl the tropics upon the waters!"

The voice of the serpent was always seductive. The jungle, inflamed, arose with a single voice:

"Yes, Anaconda! You are right! Let us fling the zone on the river! We'll go down, down!"

At last Anaconda breathed freely; her fight was won. The soul, one might say, of an entire land, with its weather, its fauna, its flora, is not easily moved; but when its nerves are taut in a frightful drought, then nothing is more certain than the good resolutions it makes for a great flood.

In her haunts, to which the great boa returned, the drought was extreme.

"Well?" the suffering beasts queried. "Is the other basin with us? Will it rain again, tell us? Are you sure, Anaconda?"

"I am. Before this moon wanes we shall hear the clouds roll in the hills. Water, brothers, and for no short season!"

To that magic voice, water! the entire jungle clamoured a desperate echo:

"Water! Water!"

"Yes, and mighty! But we must not stampede

248

when it roars. We have invaluable allies, and they will send us messengers when the moment comes. Scan the sky constantly, to the northeast. The toucans will fly from there. When they come, we have won. Till then, patience."

But how require beings whose skins are splitting from sheer drought, whose eyes are blood-shot, whose lithe trot is become an aimless drag, to have patience?

Day after day, the sun rose upon the mud with intolerable brightness, and sank smothered in bloody mists, merciless. At nightfall, Anaconda would glide to the Paranahyba to sense in the shadows the slightest quiver of rain from the implacable north. The less exhausted animals had dragged themselves to the coast. Together, they would all pass the nights without hunger or sleep, inhaling, like life itself, the least smell of moist soil in the breeze.

Till one night, the miracle occurred. Unmistakable, the presaging wind brought to these creatures a slight breath of wet leaves.

"Water! Water!" The cry went up again in the desolate valley. And joy reigned indeed five hours later, when at dawn, in the silence, the distant dull roar of the jungle under the storm was heard at last.

That morning the sun shone, not yellow but orange, and at noon was obliterated. And the rain came, dense, packed, white as oxidized silver, and drenched the parched soil.

Ten days and ten nights the tempest closed down on the jungle that floated in mists; the great bowl of intolerable light had become a sheet glistening to the horizon. Aquatic growths spread in green mats that could be seen swelling into each other. And when nine days had gone with no word from the northeast, disquiet again stole in on the waiting crusaders.

"They will never come!" was the cry. "Let us go, Anaconda! Soon it will be too late. The rains will stop."

"And begin again. Patience, little brothers! It must rain there! The toucans fly badly; they say so themselves. Likely they are on the way now. Two days more!"

But Anaconda was not nearly so certain as she seemed. What if the toucans were lost in the mists of the steaming jungle? What if by incredible disaster, the northeast rains had not matched the northwest? Half a day away, the Paranahyba thundered brimming with the cataracts of its tributaries.

As if watching for the dove of the ark, the worried beasts kept their eyes fixed to the northeast, toward the sky where their great plan must begin. Nothing. Till in a gust of fog, the toucans arrived, wet, terrified, cawing:

"Great rains! Rain all over the valley! It's all white with the rain!"

And a savage howl surged through the jungle.

"Down! The victory is ours! Down we go!"

It was time, one might say, because the Paranahyba was overflowing even its own bed, beyond its course. From river to lagoon, the swamps were now a tranquil sea, rippled by young logs. To the north, under the weight of the overflow, the green sea yielded suavely, described a great curve licking the bush, and bent gently south, sucked by the swift current.

The hour was come. The militant jungle filed before the eyes of Anaconda. Blooms born yesterday and old reddish crocodiles, ants and jaguars, tree-trunks and snakes, foam, turtles, fevers, and the very air disgorging rain—the entire jungle passed down, hailing the boa, toward the abyss of great floods.

Then when Anaconda had watched her fill, she in turn let herself be drawn, floating, to the Paranahyba: cradled in a bodily uprooted cedar which descended whirling in the eddies, she sighed at last and with a smile, closed her glazed eyes to the sunset.

She was content.

Began the miraculous voyage to the unknown, for she had no vision of what could lie beyond the rose-coloured rocks that rising from the Guayra shut off the river. Through the Tacuarí she had once reached the basin of the Paraguay. Of the middle and lower Paraná, she knew nothing.

Serene, however, in full view of the tropic that descended triumphantly adance on the channelled waters, refreshed in mind and by rain, the great serpent rode swinging down the deluge.

She descended thus her native Paranahyba,

glimpsed the subsiding whirls as she left the Rio Muerto, and barely came back to consciousness when the entire floating jungle, and the cedar, and she herself, were hurled through the foam at the gradient of the Guayra, where its ladder-leaps sank at last into a slanting chasm. For a long time the strangled river churned its red waters to the depths. But two laps ahead the banks spread out again, and the stream, filmed as oil, without a twist or a murmur flowed through the trough at nine miles an hour.

To a new land, new climate. Limpid heavens now and radiant sun, veiled barely a moment by morning vapours. Anaconda, like a very young serpent, opened her eyes curiously upon a day in Misiones,* recalling confusedly, almost forgetting, her earliest youth.

She turned to see the beach rise and float with the first ray of the sun, out of a milky fog that dissolved bit by bit, and hung in shadowy coves, streaming from the wet prows of pirogues. She felt again,

---

* A locality in the Argentine Chaco, and the scene of another tale about Anaconda.

as she swept into the great pools where the flow was interrupted, that giddiness of water whirling before her eyes in smooth, dizzy curves, boiling against the current, bubbling reddened to blood. And in the afternoons, over and over she watched the sun weld again great flaming fans, the center crimson and vibrant, while far above white spirals wandered alone, pocked everywhere with fiery sparks.

It was all familiar, but hazily, as in a dream. Sensing, especially at night, the warm pulse of the flood that descended too, the boa rode on, then suddenly coiled with a disturbed jerk.

The cedar had rammed into something strange, or at least rare in the river.

No one ignores how much is dragged, along the surface or half submerged, in a great flood. Several times already animals unknown even to Anaconda, drowned far to the north, had floated past, to sink slowly under a flapping cloud of avid crows. She had seen hundreds of snails that crawled to the highest boughs rocked by the current, shattered by the beaks of fowls. In the splendor of the moon she had watched great fish cruise up the river with their dorsal fins cutting through the water, and disappear all at once with the crash of a volley.

This was the way of the great floods.

But what had just run into her was a shelter from two waters, perhaps the fallen roof of a hut dragged by the torrent on a log raft.

A hut built insecurely on a swamp float, and undermined by the waters?   Occupied perhaps by some refugee?

Infinitely careful, scale by scale, Anaconda moved to explore the floating island.   It was occupied indeed, and under the thatch lay a man.   But he had a wide gash in his throat, and he was dying.

For a long time, without stirring even the tip of her tail a fraction, Anaconda gazed upon her enemy.

In this same great gulf of the river, walled by sandy rose cliffs, she had first known man.   Of that meeting she retained no clear memory; only a feeling of distaste, a great revulsion of herself, every time chance, and only chance, brought back a vague detail of that adventure.

Friends again, never. Enemies, obviously, since the struggle was turned against them.

Nevertheless Anaconda did not move; and the hours went by. It was still dark when the great serpent suddenly uncoiled, and went to the edge of the raft with her head toward the black waters.

The odor of fish meant snakes in the neighborhood.

And indeed clumps of them were coming.

"What is the matter?" Anaconda asked. "You know quite well that you should not desert your logs in a flood."

"We know it," the intruders answered. "But there is a man here. He is an enemy of the jungle. Make way, Anaconda."

"What for? There is no right of way. That man is wounded. . . . He is dead."

"And what do you care? If he isn't dead, he will be pretty soon. . . . Make way, Anaconda!"

The great boa reared, arching her neck.

"I have said that no one passes! Back! I have taken the sick man under my protection. Beware, whoever goes near him!"

The Return of Anaconda

"Beware yourself!" the snakes whistled shrilly, filling their murderous fangs.

"Beware of what?"

"Of what you do. You have sold yourself to man! Long-tailed lizard!"

Hardly had the rattlesnake hissed that last word, when the boa's head like a terrible battering-ram had crushed it, and left it to float, dead, its belly limp to the sky.

"Beware!" And the boa's voice rose to a screech. "Not a snake will be left in all of Misiones if a single one of you advances! Bought, I! . . . you scoundrels! To the water! And remember: night or day, I will not have snakes around that man. Understand?"

"Understood!" the sombre voice of a yararacusú * spoke from the shadows. "But some day, Anaconda, we shall call you to account for this."

"Once," answered Anaconda, "I rendered account to one of you. . . . And she wasn't satisfied. Beware yourself, beautiful *yarará*! And now, watch yourselves! . . . And a pleasant voyage!"

* A great reptile.

Somehow Anaconda was not satisfied. Why had she done this? What bound or could ever bind her to that man—an unfortunate peasant, apparently—dying with his throat laid open?

Dawn came.

"Bah!" the great boa murmured finally, gazing for the last time at the wounded man. "He is not worth bothering about. . . . Some poor devil, like all the others, and with only an hour to live. . . ."

And with a disdainful switch of her tail, she curled up in the center of her floating isle.

But all day long her eyes never left the logs.

Dark had barely set in, when high mounds of ants, washed along on a hull of millions of drowned ants, floated toward the raft.

"We are the ants, Anaconda," they said, "and we come to reproach you. That man on his heap of straw is an enemy of ours. We do not see him, but the snakes know he is there. They have seen him, and the man is asleep under the roof. Kill him, Anaconda."

"No, sisters. Go in peace."

"Let the snakes kill him, then."

The Return of Anaconda

"Nor that. Do you know the laws of the floods? This raft is mine, and I am upon it. Peace, ants."

"But the snakes have told everybody. . . . They say you have sold yourself to men. . . . Don't be angry, Anaconda."

"And who believes it?"

"No one, that is true. . . . Only the jaguars are dissatisfied."

"Ah! . . . And why don't they come and tell me themselves?"

"We do not know, Anaconda."

"I do know. Well, little sisters, go now in peace, and see that not all of you drown, because pretty soon you will be needed badly. Don't worry about your Anaconda. Now and always, I am and shall be the faithful child of the jungle. Tell them that. Goodnight, comrades."

"Goodnight, Anaconda!" the little ants answered quickly. And the dark swallowed them.

Anaconda had proved her loyalty and intelligence often enough to insure the jungle's love and respect for her against a viperine slander. Though her scant liking for rattlers and all kinds of snakes was no secret to anybody, still they played so indispensable a part in the flood that the boa herself swam out in great circles to conciliate them.

"I seek no quarrel," she said to the snakes. "As much as yesterday, and as long as the campaign lasts, I belong in body and soul to the flood. Only, the raft is mine, and I shall do as I please with it. That is all."

The snakes did not answer a word. As if they heard nothing, they did not even turn their cold eyes to the speaker.

"Bad sign!" the flamingoes croaked all together from a distance, as they watched the meeting.

"Bah!" whined the dripping crocodiles as they climbed on a tree-trunk. "Let Anaconda alone. . . . Whims of hers. And the man must be dead by now."

But the man would not die. To the amazement of Anaconda, three more days had gone and had not taken with them the last gasp of the dying man. She did not desert her post an instant; but although the snakes no longer approached, other doubts troubled Anaconda.

The Return of Anaconda

She calculated—all water serpents know more hydrography than any man—that they must now be near the Paraguay. And without the fantastic fleets of logs that river drags in its great floods, the struggle was ended at the beginning. What did the green patches that the Paranahyba bore amount to, compared with the 180,000 square kilometers of logs lifted from the huge swamps of Xarayes? The jungle that floated with her knew her reckoning too, from her own accounts of it when she crusaded. So thatch hut, wounded man and grudges were all submerged in the common anxiety of the crusaders, who hour after hour searched the waters for the allied reinforcements.

"And if the toucans," Anaconda thought, "have made a mistake, and precipitately heralded what was nothing but a miserly drizzle?"

"Anaconda!" From several directions came voices in the shadows. "Don't you recognize those waters yet? Have they deceived us, Anaconda?"

"I don't think so," the boa would answer sombrely. "Another day, and the logs of the Paraguay shall join us."

"Another day! We are losing all our strength in this stretch of the river! Still a day! You always say the same thing, Anaconda!"

"Patience, brothers! I suffer more than you do."

The next day was hard, made still worse by the dry surroundings, and the boa endured it immobile and watchful on her floating island, which flamed in the sunset glow that stretched like a bar of molten metal across the river, travelling with her.

In the dark that same night, Anaconda, who for hours had been swimming among the rafts anxiously tasting the waters, suddenly gave a cry of triumph.

She had just discovered, in an immense drift, the salty flavour of logs from the Olidén.

"Saved, brothers!" she exclaimed. "The Paraguay descends with us! Great rains there too!"

And the spirit of the jungle, revived miraculously, acclaimed the adjacent flood, whose rafts, packed thick as solid earth, pushed into the Paraná.

Next day the sun shone on that epic union of the two great systems.

The sweep of aquatic growth flowed, welded into

wide islands that covered the river. The voice of
the jungle rose as one, when the logs nearest the
bank, drawn by a dead water, whirled uncertainly,
their direction undetermined.

"Make way! Make way!" The entire flood
pulsed in the face of the obstacle. And the rafts
and logs, pressed by the load of the attackers, escaped
the suction at last, and filed off at a tangent.

"On! Make way! Make way!" could be heard
from one bank to the other. "We have won!"

Anaconda believed it also. Her dream was about
to come true. And swollen with pride she cast a
triumphant glance toward the shadow of the hut.

The man was dead. He had not moved, not a
finger was turned, not even the mouth was closed.
But he was quite dead; perhaps had been so for several hours.

Though this was to be expected and more than
natural, Anaconda was astounded, as if the lowly
mensú, notwithstanding his breed and his wounds,
should have preserved for her his humble spark of
life.

What did she care about that man! She had defended him, surely; she had shielded him from the snakes, watching over and sustaining, in the flood itself, one bit of hostile life.

Why? She did not care. There he might remain, under that shelter, without another thought from her. She had new fears.

For the fate of the great flood was menaced by a danger unforeseen by her. The weed, crushed in the long wash through heated waters, was beginning to ferment. Large bubbles oozed to the surface through the growth, and limp seeds adhered in patches all around it. For a moment, between high banks, the jungle had completely covered the river, till no water could be seen at all, only a great green sea throughout the channel. But now, the low banks could no longer contain the deluge, and the water, with the drive of its first days exhausted, languished over the drowned interior which, like a trap, spread a level before it.

Still farther down, the great rafts broke here and there, without the power to pass still pools, and were marooned in deep bays with their portent of fecundity. Lulled and sweetened, the logs yielded softly to the cross-currents along the banks, rose gently with them up the Paraná in two great curves, and settled at last to mould along the beach.

The boa too had been caught in the fruitful languor that seeped through the flood. She went from one end to the other of her floating island, quieted nowhere. Near her, almost beside her, the dead man decomposed. Anaconda approached constantly, breathed, as in a jungle niche, the heat of ferment, and trailed her warm belly over the waters, as in the days of her earliest youth.

But that water, now too fresh, was not propitious. The dead man lay in the shadow of the thatch. Might not that death be more than the sterile oblivion of the being she had guarded? And would there be nothing, nothing left to her of him?

Inch by inch, and deliberate as if before a natural shrine, Anaconda wreathed her coils. And by the side of the man she had defended as she would have her own life, within the fruitful heat of his decay —posthumous gratitude which the jungle only might have understood—Anaconda began to lay her eggs.

The flood was defeated. No matter how vast the companion basins, no matter how violent the wash, the passion of its vegetation had burned down the vigor of the torrent. Logs still floated past, but the heartening cry, "Make way! Make way!" was completely silenced.

Anaconda dreamed no more.

She was certain of the disaster. She felt upon them the vast flat space into which the flooded logs would wane, not having closed the river. Faithful to the heat of the rotting man, she continued to lay her living eggs, without the least hope for herself.

Now infinitely through cold waters, the rafts of logs dismembered and scattered over the surface. Long, rounded waves played wantonly with the torn jungle, whose land inhabitants, bewildered and still, sank stiff in the chill sea.

Large boats—the victors—trailed smoke in the distance over the clear sky, and a little steamer waving white plumes pried about among the broken rafts. Still farther away, in blue space, Anaconda reared, silhouetted, up on her isle, and her robust ten meters through the distance caught the gaze of the sightseers.

"Yonder!" a voice on the boat cried suddenly. "On the raft! An enormous snake!"

"What a monster!" shouted another voice. "And look! There is a fallen hut! It has surely murdered the owner!"

"Or devoured him alive! Those giants are merciless. Let us avenge the wretch with a speedy bullet."

"Be careful, not too near!" the first one shouted again. "The monster must be furious! It might even attack us the minute it saw us. Can you aim from here?"

"We shall see. . . . It won't hurt to try. . . ."

In the rising sun that gilded the green-speckled bay, Anaconda had seen the launch with its trailing crest. She was looking indifferently at it, when she saw a little puff of smoke at the prow—and her head struck against the timbers of the raft.

The boa reared herself again, wondering. She had felt a dry little blow somewhere on her body, perhaps in her head. She could not understand why.

And yet she knew something had happened to her. She felt her body drowsy, first; and then the need to sway her neck, as if the world, and not her head, had begun to dance, and to darken.

She saw in front of her her native bush vividly landscaped, but upside down; and through it, the smiling house of the dead *mensú*.

"I am very sleepy . . ." Anaconda thought, still trying to open her eyes. Bluish and enormous, her eggs filled the shelter and overflowed, covering the entire raft.

"It must be time to sleep . . ." Anaconda murmured. And thinking to lay her head softly upon her eggs, she flattened it out forever.

THE END